IN LOVE WITH A HEARTBREAKER

In Love with a Heartbreaker

Ben Akponine-Samuel

Published in 2023 by Tamarind Hill Press

ISBN Paperback: 978-1-915161-87-1
ISBN eBook: 978-1-915161-88-8

Tamarind Hill Press Limited
Copies are available at special rates for bulk orders. Contact us on email at business@tamarindhillpress.com or by phone on +44 1325 775 255
OR +44 7982 90 90 37 (WhatsApp) for more information.

TAMARiND HiLL .PRESS

www.tamarindhillpress.com

DEDICATION

To the evergreen memory of Prince Olusola Raphael Lewis.

CONTENTS

CHAPTER 1

Boma Horsfall sat impatiently in the living room, staring blankly at the television set. Her elder sister, Tonye, was busy talking to her elder brother, Abiye. Tonye was actually explaining the storyline of the film she was watching. Abiye was listening attentively. He was standing by the couch, dressed smartly in a white-striped light blue shirt and a pair of black jeans trousers. He was obviously set to go out that evening, possibly to a club. Boma sighed silently for the third time.

Just then, Abiye looked at his wristwatch and he too sighed. "This guy is wasting my time," he said and paced towards another couch. He quickly returned his attention to Tonye who had not stopped her narration despite the interruption.

Boma was silent. Her mind was in a riot. She became uncomfortable. Getting up, Boma left the living room. She went upstairs to her room. Until recently, she'd shared the room with her sister. Tonye had moved downstairs to one of the guestrooms and had taken it as hers. The upstairs room provided Boma a view of outside. She would see him when he came.

Her heart beat seemed to increase. Why had he not come? Her brother was downstairs waiting for him. What was keeping him? Was he with one of the numerous girls she had heard he frolicked about with? Her heart shook and she hoped against the thought. Maybe he was being delayed by traffic? Where was he even coming from? She had heard her brother telling Tonye that he was coming to pick him up, and at that moment, she had gotten very anxious and impatient. She wanted to see him again.

Richard!

She had met him only once a few days ago and from that brief meeting, he had become very significant in her mind that she had woven so many crazy thoughts around him. She had even imagined, joyfully, that he was walking her down the aisle. He was so handsome; the most handsome man she had ever met at such close proximity and it seemed, gratefully, that he would be around for a while. She had fallen in love, and helplessly so, with him.

She had just returned from school a week ago after staying away for a full year. Boma had just wanted to be away in school since she had no reason to come home. Her father had provided her a good and comfortable accommodation just off-campus and it was home to her. She had everything. Her mother had visited a couple of times. If not for Christmas and the pressure from her father to come home, she would have stayed even through the holidays. She would be done by midyear and would become a graduate.

Now, she was glad she came back. That was the day she met Richard. The driver had picked her up from the airport and brought her home. Her brother was outside in the compound with this gorgeous young man whose sight almost snatched the breath out of her. He was tall, broad shouldered even though with a slender frame yet athletic build. He was a good head over her brother whom she had always considered very tall.

Abiye had embraced her as soon as she had alighted from the car. He was very happy to see her. His friend stood a bit aloof, his hands in his pocket, staring and smiling as if he was waiting to be introduced.

Abiye began to help her carry her load. He did not bother to introduce her to his gorgeous friend. She could not ask her brother who he was or to be introduced to him. She felt uneasy.

"Hello," the young man said, coming up to her, beaming the most charming smile she had thought was ever flashed at her. "My name is Richard and I think you are worth meeting. You're such a goddess!" He extended his hand.

She was about to take his hand and tell him her name but her brother had yelled and run in between them. "What is going on here? She is my kid sister. You don't need to meet her," Abiye protested, shoving his friend aside and wagging a finger at him. "I don't like it."

Richard had burst into laughter. "What is your problem? Can't I meet your sister? Haven't I met Tonye?" he asked, amused.

"No, don't meet her. She is not in your league," Abiye said.

Boma felt a bit embarrassed. "Let him be, Abiye," she muttered.

"You heard her. She said you should let me be," Richard said, almost triumphantly.

Abiye looked at her and shook his head. "You don't know this guy. He is my friend from secondary school and we went to the same university. He just moved to town because his bank sent him here," he said. "He's dangerous!"

"Patrick, do not scandalize me before this beautiful angel," Richard said, calling Abiye by the English name he answered to in school and on his official documents. However, he was Abiye at home. He was the only one who had a western name in the family because she and Tonye had no such names. "What's your name?" he asked her.

"Boma," she said before her brother could stop her. He was obviously joking with his friend but underneath that joke, he was serious and even his friend knew that.

"Wow! Such an angelic name for the most beautiful goddess eyes ever saw," Richard said.

"Shut up!" Abiye said to him as he dragged her into the house where they met Tonye who was rushing out to meet her. The sisters hugged. That had been a week ago and Boma had been thinking of Richard since that day and even missed him. He had become the most important person to her heart in these few days. She had not seen him again after that day.

Richard is very handsome. He would be the perfect man for me, she had thought. She was building dreams around him despite what her brother had said about him.

"That guy is not a serious person when it comes to ladies. He is an unrepentant heart breaker. Girls easily fall in love with him because he is handsome and has a sugar-coated tongue. He knows how to blow a woman's head by paying her obsequious compliments. He has always been like that from secondary school days. Girls fight over him and he ends up messing them up," Abiye had said.

"Messing them up? How?" she had asked, feigning disgust.

"He breaks their hearts. It was worse in university. There wasn't a month when a girl did not cry because Richard had dumped her for another girl. Very crazy! I don't want him close to my sisters," he had explained.

Boma had felt heartbroken at the story but then, it was for a moment. The thought of him excited her and she kept dreaming about him.

CHAPTER 2

Boma saw him when he alighted from the car that pulled up in front of her house gates. He looked beautiful even in the late evening light. Her heart suddenly began to race with excitement. She hurried out of the room and almost flew down the stairs. She startled her siblings when she dashed into the living room in such a hurry.

"He's here. He's coming in," she blurted out in excitement.

Her brother and sister's bewildered stares at her made her realize herself. And that was an awkward moment for her. She was deflated. She walked to a couch and sank into it; her brother's eyes still following her.

"Who's here?" he asked.

"I thought you wanted to go out with your friend and you have been waiting for him?" she replied.

The door of the living room slid open and Boma almost jumped. Her mother entered the room. She asked them what they were watching. Tonye began to tell her. Tonye always found relish in narrating stories to whoever was ready to hear. Boma noticed that her brother was still staring at her. She grimaced at him to hide her discomfort. She could tell he had his suspicion.

Just then, the door slid open again. This time, Boma made concerted effort not to look. She kept her face straight, staring at the television, even though she was not seeing it. Richard's voice boomed as he entered, greeting her mother. It was obvious that he had become familiar with her family.

"How are you, Richie?" her mother asked.

"I am doing great, Mum," he replied. She was surprised. He called her mother Mum! She noticed her brother looked at her but she did not flinch.

"Hello Richie Boy!" Tonye said, stressing the word boy and sounding jocular. She actually laughed.

"Tonye, the most beautiful princess in the world," Richard said.

"Liar!" Tonye responded. "Your flattery won't get you anywhere."

Richard laughed. "But jokes apart, you always look ravishingly beautiful, Tonye. Everybody in the world knows this fact," he said.

Tonye hissed jokingly.

A louder hiss came from Abiye. “She already told you it won’t get you anywhere. Get that into your skull. Why did you keep me waiting?”

“Sorry, I took Barbara home,” Richard said.

“Who is Barbara?” Tonye asked exactly what Boma was thinking. “Another victim?”

“That’s the right question. Another victim?” Abiye said and laughed.

Abiye’s mother looked at Richard. “I don’t want to believe what I am hearing,” she said.

“Mum, don’t mind them. That is how they tease me. I am a good guy,” Richard said.

Boma could no longer bear keeping her face averted. She had expected that he would look her way and throw a greeting at her but the wait seemed never ending. The moment her head moved to look at him, their eyes met.

“Hi Boma,” he threw at her and turned to her brother. “Let’s go!”

Boma’s heart dropped to the pit of her stomach and cracked. *Hi Boma!* his voice reverberated in her head. What did he mean by just that? She meant nothing to him! She was more or less a nobody to him. She was hurt. This was a man she had been crushing after and longing to see all week and he gave her a very negligible notice. He had paid glowing compliments to Tonye and she had thought he would do the same to her.

She rose and left the living room. Thankfully, her mother and sister had their attention on the television set. She went upstairs to her room. She felt weak and spent. Who was Barbara? His girlfriend? Was she as beautiful as Boma was?

Boma laid in bed, exhausted by the disappointing snub she got from Richard. Maybe, she was right after all, love was not for her. She had vowed when she was in her first year at university that she would never allow herself to ever fall in love again and get hurt. This was after George. She heaved a heavy sigh. She did not want to think of George. She had long put him behind her. His many entreaties to win her back for more than a year had hit the brick wall because she had made a vow.

Now, here she was again, with Richard, having nothing between them except that she had helplessly fallen in love with him even at first sight, not minding his dangerous faults, yet she obviously had not occurred to him. She had nothing with him yet she was heartbroken like a jilted lover.

***

George was cute. He was bulky, fresh like a well-fed kid, a complexion on the light side; he was handsome and was a major toast amongst many students on campus. He cut a class as a campus celebrity. Girls simply called him Fine Boy George after the English music sensation. It was near impossible to be at that university and not know who George or FBG as he was later simply called was. He was obviously a rich boy from his mere appearance. His father was a two time minister and a former ambassador. So, George had everything going for him.

He was in his third year when Boma entered the school. Her older sister had told her to beware of boys who would swoop on the freshers with the assumption that they were still naive, ignorant, and innocent. Armed with that advice, she was ready not to cave in to any boy's gambit.

In her first week on campus, she heard stories about George, touted to be one of the most handsome and most influential students on campus. She heard that he drove an exotic car, which he changed every semester. *He must be very rich,* was her first thought of him.

"That is the kind of guy I like," Sophia, a freshman who was her new friend and also her roommate had said when Belema, a second year student had told them about George.

"Why?" Boma had asked, surprised at Sophia's words. "Is it because he is popular?"

"That is just an added one. The fact that he is handsome and rich means he can take care of me and make me feel good always," Sophia said.

"The guy is every girl's crush. You just need to set eyes on him," Belema said.

"Anyway, I am not in school to have relationships. I have always been a good girl. I've had boys hot after me in secondary school but I never gave any a chance," Boma said.

"Well, this is university, an adult centre," Belema said.

Three days later, the three girls were returning from the school library to their hostel when a flashy car pulled up in front of them. Belema became excited.

"That is George," she exclaimed, acknowledging the flashy car.

George stepped out of the car. He was wearing a white tee-shirt with a pair of jeans trousers and white trainers. He looked very clean; he stared at them, beaming.

"I can swear it is you he's smiling at, Boma. You are the most beautiful here," Belema said under her breath as they walked towards him.

"It could be anybody," Sophia said. She had suddenly changed her steps and seemed to be wriggling her waist as she walked rather seductively. They were almost walking past him when he raised his hand, his smile pasted on his face.

"Hello. Excuse me," he said to them.

Sophia stepped towards him. “Yes? What can I do for you?”

“Sorry, not you,” he said. He pointed to Boma, “You, please.”

Sophia was obviously deflated. She walked on, dragging Belema along.

“What can I do for you? You see my friends are already leaving me,” she said.

He nodded. “I won’t waste your time, but please, just tell me where I can find you later this evening. Your hostel or anywhere you would be,” he said.

“What for?” she asked with a grimace. Her eyes were tough. She was light complexioned and she did not really like boys of her complexion. The few boys she had ever admired, albeit secretly, were always the dark complexioned ones.

CHAPTER 3

George broke Boma's heart in just under six months. She had not seen it coming even though she had heard stories of his exploits. She had just paid little attention to what she heard about him.

That fateful evening, led by Sophia and another of her friends, Dani, she had gone to the bar just outside the campus and found him there necking openly and without shame or any iota of respect for her with another girl, Tombra. Tombra was a popular campus big girl with a cheery happy-go-lucky mien.

George saw her and smiled as if everything was okay. Tombra pulled him back to her and buried his head in her huge cleavage, laughing loud like someone without a care in the world. George made no effort to resist her. Boma was shattered. She could not afford to have a showdown with Tombra knowing her character and dreading the possibility of her getting bitchy if she made any attempt to spoil her fun. She turned and walked away; her friends at the door went with her.

"That boy is no good. He is a player," Sophia said rather triumphantly.

"A spoilt womanizer and heart breaker," Dani added.

Boma offered no word. She was hurting as she returned to her hostel. She ran herself a bath as soon as she got to her room. In the bathroom, she broke down and wept. George had dealt her a terrible blow. She loved him and had accepted him, believing that all would be fine and he had shown no sign that he would cheat on her. She finished her bath and went straight to bed, weakened by the betrayal.

Even though she had gone to bed early that night, she could not sleep as she laid awake far into the night, her heart in smithereens. She regretted the day she met George.

Boma had always been a beautiful girl, light complexioned, pretty face with childish sweetness and softness, almost cherubic. She was taller than average and was also a bit more than average in weight. She had an hourglass shape with an almost massive hip, a prominent feature that made her more desirable and a major source of masculine attraction from the time she had begun to bloom. A male teacher in secondary school had once described her as nubile, and upon looking up the meaning, she had been offended and had reported it to her mother. Though she regretted that action because the teacher got sacked for such description of a teenage girl when her mother had stormed the school in anger. She had since then become aware of her sex appeal. As she grew, she blossomed and it was apparent that the opposite sex found her irresistible.

Now, she felt spent and wasted because the first boy she had ever given her heart to had dealt her a massive blow. George had pestered her for months to accept him. He was everywhere after her. Sometimes, he would just drop by her hostel with gifts for her. He was so nice and sweet to her. He stopped talking about trying to date her. He was just being nice to her.

On her birthday, he gave her a surprise party. She did not know how he even found out that it was her birthday. That had melted her heart towards him and she believed he was the man for her. She spent that night thinking about him and then she was ready to explore love with him. The next time he broached the issue of dating her, she did not disappoint him again. He seemed the happiest man in the world.

George had treated her like a queen. He was always there for her. He flaunted her to everyone and in such a short time, they had become an item. He constantly professed love to her and she had completely fallen.

It was the moments of their lives; they basked in their love. It was so steamy and she wanted more. He meant the world to her.

“Why do they call you Fine Boy George?” she asked him one day when they were taking a walk towards her hostel. He had come to her faculty to walk her back to her hostel. He did that most times when he was not having a lecture. He knew her timetable.

“You know the British musician Boy George who was the lead singer of the Culture club?” he asked.

She had grimaced and then, her face contorted in disgust. “And you are happy to be called after him? I don’t think I like him. He’s queer and weird and he’s androgynous in his looks,” she said remembering how her brother, Abiye had once described the musician. Her brother was a strong hater of Boy George but her sister loved him and his music.

“What is that? Androgen, or what did you say?” George had asked.

“Androgynous. Androgyny is having a mix of feminine and masculine features in an indistinct form. That is what Boy George does. He is a man but he blends the female characteristics with the male and looks like it. I hear he is queer,” she said.

“Queer as in gay?” George asked.

“Yes. And I don’t like it that you go by that name. You are George; that is fine. Remove the Boy. Fine George is okay, after all, Boy signifies immaturity,” she had said.

He had chewed over it and then let out a hard sigh. "I honestly know very little about him. I don't even know his songs. Someone just told me that he is a very popular English musician and people love him, so I just thought it was cool. I won't let anyone call me that name again. George is just fine," he had said.

She had laughed and he laughed too. And just like that, he stopped people from calling him anything other than his name. He was no longer FBG. Boma was happy because she thought she had a good effect on him and he must love her so much to accept to change the name he had been used to being called long before he knew her.

The girls envied her because she was the girlfriend of the boy who was in the circle of many girls' wish. She became popular.

"Well, it is your turn. Enjoy it while it last," a girl named Damiete, who was George's course-mate said to her one day in a salon on campus. She had been puzzled and asked what exactly the girl meant. "George is a rich fine boy. He is also spoilt. He may be in love with you today but that doesn't guarantee he would feel the same tomorrow," she said.

Boma's heart shook and she became scared that he would leave her. "You cannot say that for sure," she said, wondering what had even begun the discussion in the first place.

Damiete looked at her and smiled. "Anyway, you are a very beautiful girl yourself and he may finally have found a girl he truly loves but I have known George from our first year in this school. He's in my department and class. He is too spoilt and even too full of himself to stay with one girl. He changes girls as frequently as he changes his cars, every semester; that is aside his many escapades," she said.

Boma was hurt to hear this about George. When he came to pick her up from the salon later and took her to her hostel, she had been gloomy. He asked her what the matter was but she would not talk.

"You are killing me with your silence, Boma. What is the matter with you?" he asked. He pleaded with her to talk to him. He followed her into her hostel, worried that something was troubling her and was more worried that she did not want to talk to him about it.

"Boma, you know I love you and don't want anything to disturb you. Please, I am begging you, share with me what is bothering you? Did someone offend you?" he asked, actually pleading.

She looked at him. She saw a different person from what Damiete had painted. This was a caring George who loved her and he was worried because she was not talking. How could this be the frightening monster Damiete had made her picture back at the salon?

"Will you ever leave me, George?" she asked.

He was shocked. “Leave you? Why?” he asked, his stupefaction written all over him.

“Answer my question,” Boma said, not ready for any drama.

“Not for a thousand worlds would I ever leave you. As long as I am alive, I will never leave you,” he said.

“But you change girls every now and then,” she replied. It was a direct accusation.

“Yes, it is true. I change girls every now and then,” he admitted.

That crushed her. She stared at him in disbelief. Maybe a denial would have made her feel better. She was speechless as tears welled up in her. She held herself from flickering her eyelids to avoid the tears from pouring down.

“I have my reasons. All the girls I have dated in this school came to me. They asked me out; they begged me to date them. It’s not like I fell in love with any of them. There was no excitement, no chemistry, there was nothing. I will naturally get tired and move on. But you are different. The moment I saw you, I fell in love, truly in love. You are the perfect beauty of my dream. I came after you and you gave me a tough time but I did not give up because I truly love you. That is why you made me a better person. You matter so much to me. You are my choice and I love you. So, why would I leave you for anything?” he explained.

It was a sigh of relief that came upon her and her eyes flickered. The tears flowed down but they were different tears, no longer of the pains that created them but of the reassurance that his words gave her. She believed him. She hugged him tight. "I love you too, George. Please, don't you ever leave me," she said.

"I will never," he assured her.

CHAPTER 4

Boma finally nodded off. She felt really exhausted. The night was, however, fractured with many vague dreams of George and his betrayal. She tossed about the bed, breaking sleep and then going back to the same pattern. It was a very horrendous night and when she woke up a few hours later to empty her bladder, sleep eluded her. The thoughts assailed her again. George had done the worst to her!

He did not even come after her. What difference would it have made, though? She had caught him red-handed and that was it. Many thoughts crashed into her mind. The same George who had assured her of his undying love for her and who had said so many sweet lies just to deceive her. Why had she trusted him so much?

It was Sophia who had first told her that George was a serial cheater. She had not paid any attention to her more because Belema had advised her that if she wanted her relationship with George to be meaningful, she must never listen to any gossip. Sophia told her that she saw him in an eatery in town with a tall beautiful dark complexioned girl.

“Sophia, she could be his family member or just a friend,” Boma had told her.

“That girl cannot be his family. They look so different and the way he was holding her around her waist did not suggest anything of family ties or platonic friendship,” Sophia said.

Boma had ignored her. Then three more times, Sophia had come with stories of seeing George with different girls.

“Why are you always the one seeing him with girls?” Belema had asked. “Are you sure you are not trying to break them up so he can be free for you to slip in?”

Sophia had been irritated. “Slip in where? With that Casanova? Never! I am just trying to protect Boma because the guy is wicked. Cheating on her is wickedness,” Sophia said. Her countenance expressed disapproval for George. It was now it had occurred to Boma that Sophia truly did not like George. Whenever he came to see her in the room, Sophia would leave without even saying a word to him.

“Sophia, thank you, but please, just channel your energies elsewhere and leave George alone,” Boma told her.

Sophia looked defeated. She shrugged weakly. “Anyway, don’t say I did not warn you,” she said.

“Mind your business,” Belema warned.

Boma had confronted George with all that she had heard and each time he would just laugh and tell her to stop listening to rumours. "Listen, Babe, whoever is telling such lies has a mission and you must be careful of such a person or people. I am not their target. You are their target. They want you to get angry and dump me so they can try to fill in your place. If it is a boy who told you this which I know it's not, then I may be the target but if it is a girl, be sure you are the target. They are jealous of you," he said when she confronted him the last time. She had thought of what Belema had said of Sophia. She believed him.

"Please, I don't want to hear any gossip," Boma began to tell Sophia. She did not understand why Sophia was bent on making her break up with him. She also remembered that Sophia had liked George in the beginning.

George had told her he was travelling to Lagos to see his mother who was in their Lagos house; he told her he would be gone for ten days. Four days later, Dani came to her room to see Belema. They were friends and course mates. Dani always teased Boma by referring to her as the fine girlfriend of a fine boy. That day, she did the same.

"Leave Boma alone," Belema said. "She is missing George." It was the truth. Boma was really missing him.

Dani looked somewhat puzzled. "Why is she missing him? Can't she go and see him?" She turned to Boma, "If you are missing him, go and see him."

Boma was shy each time the girls talked about George and that day was not any different.

"George is not in town. He travelled to Lagos some days ago. Boma is counting the days," Belema said.

"George did not travel. I saw him yesterday and even today," Dani said.

The girls were surprised. "No, it cannot be George. George went to see his mother in Lagos," Boma said.

Just then, Sophia dashed into the room. She seemed too agitated. She called Boma's name and that startled her.

"What is it?" Boma asked.

"I thought you said George travelled? He is in a bar right now with Tombra, that wild girl whom they say runs after rich men for money. They are necking and I saw them with my eyes. If you come along, you would see for yourself," Sophia cried.

Boma could not believe what she was hearing. She was sure it was not her George. Against Belema's advice to ignore the girls, Boma elected to go to the bar. Dani and Sophia went with her. Of course, Sophia was the navigator.

It was very painful. So, George had just fooled her all along. She wiped the tears from her face. She would not cry over him. *No! He does not deserve my tears,* she said to herself, steeling up. She would act as if he never existed to her and everything that happened between them was a dream she was never meant to be part of. It was that moment she vowed that she would never fall in love again. It was over.

***

Boma let out a sigh. Why was she in this situation again? Richard was breaking her heart, in fact, he had by his snub.

Hi Boma, the greeting rang in her head again and she felt a real sense of displeasure. It was just the sign for her to beware of him. Then all she had heard about Richard began to sneak into her head. He was never serious with relationships. He was an unrepentant heartbreaker! Another heartbreaker! It was the one thing she did not want and she must avoid at all cost. She must get over him. She must forget him. There was nothing between them and he had already broken her heart. She wondered how terrible it would be had there been something.

Then, there was Barbara, his latest victim. Who was she even? What was special in her that attracted him? Or was she the one who threw herself at him? Why would a girl throw away her decency and throw herself at a man? An unserious one for that matter!

Then she recalled George's confession when he finally came to beg her after she had caught him with Tombra. The plea with a confession that only made matters worse; he had slept with Sophia in the first month of their relationship because Sophia had pestered him and had wanted him to dump Boma for herself. She had walked him out of her room. She and Sophia never spoke again.

What did girls think of when they did that? Did they ever think the men would cherish or respect them? she wondered.

Richard was no different from George. Their good looks were their weapons against women and they used them very well. In George's case, his father's wealth added to it but certainly not for her because she was not from a poor background.

She rose and walked out of the room. She would go for her supper and fill her mind with something else. She had to take Richard out of her mind. He did not care about her; she was nothing to him and he was a dangerous player.

CHAPTER 5

Boma was destabilised when she heard her mother tell Tonye to include Richard's name in the names of the invited guests for the Christmas Eve house party. It was a tradition in their home to invite a few friends to have dinner and sing Christmas carol on the day before Christmas. It was usually glam and those invited always saw it as an honour.

Boma did not understand why her mother would invite Richard. He was a heartbreaker and should not be permitted to come to their home much less their special occasion.

"Richard may not have the chance. You know he has a girlfriend he might want to spend the Christmas Eve with," Tonye said.

"Just include him. I will personally send the invitation to him. He should come with his girl. They will love it here," the woman said.

Just then, Abiye walked into the kitchen to get water. His mother looked at him. “Abiye, come. We are preparing the list of people we should invite for the Christmas carol night. Do you think your friend, Richard, would like to come?” she said.

Abiye smiled. “I have already invited him and his girlfriend. They are looking forward to it.”

“Beautiful. That settles it,” his mother said. She turned to her older daughter, “So, who else should we invite? We need at least twenty five people for the night.”

Boma got up from the kitchen stool and walked out of the kitchen to the sitting room. She did not like it that her family was inviting Richard to the party. *That cold-shoulder!* she hissed in her head. Then she experienced a sudden nervousness at the thought that his girlfriend had been invited as well. She tried not to think of it but the harder she tried not to, the more she gave it further thought.

Barbara would be at her house and she would be the centre of Richard’s attention. How she wished the event would not take place. It was just a few days away. Her heart began to beat heavily with apprehension and dread. She had no idea how she would be able to stand it.

“Is your friend that important that you and Mummy are inviting him over for the Carol night?” Boma asked her brother when he returned to the living room.

Abiye turned to look at her. He grimaced as he stared at her. "Does that bother you?" he asked. His stare was apparently coloured with suspicion.

"I am just wondering how close he is to this family that he has already been invited to our special annual occasion. I did not hear of him this time last year," she said.

"Listen, Boma, Richard is my friend, my very good friend at that. I notice that you, like many girls, are swept off your feet over him. In that area, he is no good. Don't ever give it a thought because his stock in trade is to use and dump girls," he said.

Boma looked outrageous at her brother. "What are you saying? What is my business with him? Did I tell you I am interested in him?"

"You don't have to tell me that. I see it that he has an effect on you and I fear for you. His good look is just a scam," he said.

"You read me wrong, Abiye. Your friend with the bad attitude and disrespect for women from what I have heard you say of him has no effect on me. If at all there is any effect, it is of loathing. I don't like him one bit," she said, vehemently. She was even already angry.

"Calm down. You are right. I might have read you wrongly. I just want you to know that he is a good person but a very bad lover who had no regards for any woman. Any girl you see with him is just his victim," Abiye said.

She was still annoyed at her brother's assumption of her having feelings for Richard; however, she agreed that he read her wrongly. Though, beneath the layers of her consciousness, she knew that he had read her correctly.

"Anyway, you have been away for long to know that he has been around for a while and has familiarized with this family. He brought Mummy a gift on her birthday and since then, she had begun to see him as another son. Tonye, as you know, is very free with people and easily gets along with everyone. She knows of his escapades too because she knew him in secondary school too," he said.

Boma sighed. It was true. Tonye was in secondary school when Abiye was still in secondary school but he had left before Boma got in. However, she was still worried that Richard would come for the carol night, and with Barbara!

Two days later, Boma went with her brother to pick up some items from the supermarket for her mother. She had been home since her return from school and she took that as an opportunity to go out. None of her friends had returned home for Christmas yet. Not like she had many friends though.

They were on their way in when a tall, beautiful girl who looked like a live doll called Abiye's name. She was hurrying towards them. Boma was impressed by the girl's beauty. She looked every inch like a model. She walked gracefully with class and poise. The first suspicion was that she was Abiye's girlfriend. Boma had never met any of his girlfriends. Of course, she had heard about two girls in the past from Tonye but she had never met them. Was this one of the girls or just a new one?

The beautiful girl flashed a radiant smile as she fell into Abiye's embrace.

"How are you? This must be your sister from the face," the girl said.

"Yes, she is. Her name is Boma," Abiye said, putting his arm around his sister.

The lady smiled brilliantly at Boma. "Nice meeting you. You are the most beautiful girl I've ever seen. More beautiful than your sister whom I think is extremely beautiful," she said.

"Thank you," Boma said. This was a compliment she always got from both male and female admirers. It had long settled upon her that her beauty was both classy and classic. But then, the lady was very beautiful and Boma did not think she was anywhere close to her if compared. Her elegance was too upper class and sophisticated. Then, her smile shone like a million stars. *She is breath-taking,* Boma admitted.

The lady extended her hand to Boma and Boma took it. Her hand was soft and well-manicured. "I'm Barbara. I am your brother's very good friend," she said.

Boma was shocked as she stared at the lady, suddenly letting go of her hand. "Barbara?" she intoned.

"Yes, Barbara," Barbara said, looking concerned as she noticed the girl's reaction. "Is anything the matter, Darling?"

"No," Boma said as she quickly, much to her embarrassment, realised herself. "Nothing is the matter. Sorry. I was just wondering if I've ever heard the name. Are you close with my family?"

Barbara smiled. "Not really, but I am very close with your brother and I know your beautiful sister, Tonye," she said.

"Okay," Boma said. She waited for her brother to resume with his friend.

Barbara turned to Abiye and asked him why he was there and they got talking. She even went inside the supermarket with them. Boma walked slowly from behind, checking the lady out. Was this the same Barbara whom Richard was dating? The lady looked too sophisticated for Richard. If she was the same, then, it was more than probable that Richard would stick with her. That thought spurred jealousy in her and she was embarrassed upon the realisation.

CHAPTER 6

Much as Boma wanted not to think about Richard, she found herself not only thinking about him but also worrying about Barbara being his girlfriend. She dreaded that they would both come to her house on Christmas Eve. Her brother had confirmed to her that Barbara was the same lady Richard was seeing. She just could not imagine Richard leaving her. She was just too exquisite for any man not to hold very dearly.

Boma feared that she may not be able to stand seeing Richard with Barbara on the carol night. She would have to think of something that would keep her away from the 'family dinner with friends,' as her father always called it. There was no way she could evade it because as it was tradition, the family would give the first rendition of the night.

Why was she even worrying about Richard? He was nothing to her. She would have to steel herself against him and forget all about him, she told herself. He should not matter and Barbara too should not matter. Still, the thought of them would not go away. She was a prisoner of love.

Christmas Eve came and the party held. Boma was confused when she did not see Richard. In as much as she dreaded to see him, a part of her wanted to see him. However, Barbara came, looking very elegant and gorgeous but she did not look as bright as the glamour she wore. She hovered around Abiye and they spent the evening talking in low tones. Where then was Richard? Boma expected that he would come since his girlfriend was already here and she had been on the lookout. In the end, he did not show up. What was the matter?

Boma did not see Richard in the days that followed neither. She did not know why he did not come and she could not ask anyone about it. She was not fortunate to stumble on her sister or mother asking her brother why his friend did not show up; that way, she would have had an idea.

On the fourth day into the New Year, Boma was set to leave for school. She was sure that she would get over the thoughts of Richard. It was obvious to her that he was too held up with his gorgeous lady to even think anything special about her. School would occupy her mind; she was sure of that.

Abiye was to drop her at the airport since the driver had gone to work with her father earlier that morning. Abiye was not working at the moment because he was preparing to travel out of the country to further his studies. He left a construction company employment for this. Her father's choice it was.

She and Abiye had just finished loading her bags in the car booth when Abiye had a visitor. It was Richard. He looked so apologetic. Her brother looked at him and hissed.

"Abiye, I'm sorry. I've been too busy," Richard apologised.

Boma's heart froze momentarily and then began a rapid pulsation. What was he doing here? She stared straight at him but he did not seem to notice her. His attention was on Abiye.

"Since Christmas Eve?" Abiye asked. "You messed up. I left several notes at your place."

"Yes, I know. I am sorry. I had to hurry here now to see you and explain things to you," Richard said.

Abiye shrugged. "Well, as you can see, I am on my way out. I am taking my sister to the airport," he said.

It was now that Richard looked at Boma. She looked away at nothing in particular.

"Hi," Richard threw at her.

"Good morning," she said almost in a whisper. It was a voice that was emotionally suffused even though unintentionally. She opened the car door and slipped in just to escape. She heaved a heavy sigh. What was really wrong with him? What was all this throwing of hi at her? She sensed that Abiye had an issue with him but that did not concern her. It was her heart that was beating rather too fast that bothered her and then the thoughts of Richard that flooded her consciousness.

She heard him telling her brother that they would 'talk over it later that evening at the bar.' Abiye entered the car. Richard bent to look at her, he smiled at her. That instantly caused her heart to somersault within her ribcage.

"Alright, Boma, do take care of yourself and be good. Don't let those campus boys deceive you. Face your studies," he said to her.

All of a sudden, those words meant so much to her. She smiled back and waved at him as her brother began the engine. She wished he could enter the car and follow them to the airport.

"Are you fighting with your friend?" Boma asked her brother as they drove away.

Her brother hissed. "Don't mind him. Do you know he broke up with Barbara on the morning of Christmas Eve? Who does that?" he said.

Boma was shocked. She looked at him. "Isn't Barbara that exquisitely beautiful lady we met at the supermarket the other day?" she asked as if she was not sure. Her brother nodded. "But why? She is a super gorgeous lady. Any man would be ready to give an arm just to keep her to himself," she said.

Abiye laughed. "Not with Richard. He has no heart, and sometimes, I wonder if he will ever get married. Love to him is like a game of pleasure," he said.

"That is sad," she said. Her voice trailed off as she mentioned, "Poor girl."

Abiye hissed and said that Barbara was actually his friend and Richard had met her through him. The moment Richard had told him he liked the lady, he had warned him to stay away from her but Richard would not back off. Unfortunately, the chemistry clicked for Barbara and she wanted to know more about him. They stuck friendship almost instantly. Abiye was not happy because he knew his friend would hurt her in the end. He could not warn her because it would seem like he was soiling Richard's reputation.

The romance had been fierce and they seemed too into each other. For a moment, Abiye had begun to think that it was going to be something that was made in heaven. Their going was sweet and boisterous and they seemed very happy. It was such a delight to watch them but Abiye had his inner fears and he watched with bated breath all along. Then, suddenly, so abruptly without a warning, the affairs ended. Richard was the predator as usual and poor Barbara was heartbroken, shattered and almost lost her mind.

Barbara had told Abiye what had happened on Christmas Eve when she came for the carol night party. She had hoped that Richard would show up and with the intervention of Abiye, he could change his mind. Richard must have anticipated that and he had stayed away. All attempts for Abiye to meet him and appeal to him to be reasonable did not yield any result as Richard had been evasive. After a week of hard pursuit, Abiye, convinced that Richard was evading him, decided not to push any further. He talked to Barbara to put Richard behind her but the lady had said she would die if she tried because Richard meant the world to her.

"Richard is not someone you should expect to do what you wish. He does only what he wants. Take this as an opportunity to free yourself as an emotional prisoner, to move on and find a better day tomorrow. Let Richard end with this year to you. Tomorrow is a new day, a new month and a new year, make it a new life and for a new experience. Forget what will not be," Abiye had told her. He too was hurt by her own hurt. He had felt pity for her.

"You think being in love with Richard is being an emotional prisoner?" she had asked, her face worried amidst her hurt.

He had not known how to admit that to her. Of course, she had always been a prisoner of emotion from the day she fell in love with Richard. She was a prisoner of love with him because he would only torture her in the end and this was it. The only way for her to escape that torture was to exercise some sort of mental maturity; forget him and move on. It would be very hard if not almost impossible. "Every girl in this kind of a situation is a prisoner of emotion or love. Your emotions are too strong at this time and it would be hard to tell you to forget him and move on. If you can do that, it would be good for you and your sanity. You would escape both the emotional and mental torture," he had told her.

Tears had run down her face. Abiye had known that getting over Richard would not be easy for her and she had asked him if Richard had another girl. She believed that he had dumped her because he had another girl and Abiye and told her that he did not know of any.

"If I ever find out that he did this to me because of a girl, I will make sure that girl too goes through pains," Barbara had sworn.

Until today, Abiye had not seen Richard and he was not pleased with him. He dropped Boma at the airport and left almost immediately.

Boma was filled with the story her brother had just told her. *Richard! He is such an emotional brute! And to think he was so handsome and captivating, only for him to be so mean and thoughtless. Such a waste of good looks,* she thought.

CHAPTER 7

"Hi Boma!" Boma heard a masculine voice behind her as she dragged her luggage out of the departure hall of the domestic airport to find a taxi. She turned and saw a tall dark complexioned boy with a muscular frame. The handsome face was very familiar but she could not quickly place it.

"Hello," she muttered, her face lighting up with a smile as she tried to remember his face.

"Dele," he volunteered as he noticed her situation.

As soon as he mentioned his name, it hit home. He was a student in the same university with her. She remembered a particular rainy day when she was still in her first year and was still with George. She had been caught up at her faculty block by the rain and had been waiting when he had come along. He saw her and smiled at her.

"You must be Boma," he had said.

She had smiled back at him out of courtesy. She had also noticed his good looks even though she did not let that mean anything to her. She had George and he was everything to her at that time. He had quickly introduced himself as Dele and told her he knew her because she was George's girlfriend. He offered to drop her at her hostel in his car. She was grateful.

On their way, he had told her he was in her faculty but in a different department and also in his first year. She could tell he had his eyes on her as he kept complimenting her beauty all through. He dropped her off and she saw him once afterwards but he had seemed in a hurry and he did not wait to chat with her. It was difficult to think he was in the same faculty with her because she never saw him after that second meeting again until now.

"What are you doing here?" she asked.

"I dropped my mother off. She is going to Lagos and I decided to just take a walk around," he said. He looked happy to see her.

"Oh! Really? I am just back from the Christmas holiday and I'm off to school. I just want to take a taxi," she said.

"Don't bother about airport taxis, they are unnecessarily expensive. Why don't I drop you off at school," he offered, reaching to take one of her bags.

She was pleased. She thanked him and he led her to the carpark where his car was. Shortly, they were driving out.

"I haven't seen you since my hundred level days," she said.

He smiled. "Well, I see you always even up till early last month," he said,

She was surprised. "Really? I had no idea because I never saw you," she said.

"Yes, I know. I was actually always staying out of your sight. It was deliberate, though. I just needed to stay alive," he said.

Boma was confused. "I don't understand. What are you saying?"

Dele heaved a hard sigh. "You see, that day I gave you a lift to your hostel, some people saw me, and that night, they paid me a visit in my room. They beat me, threatening to kill me. They said I must not dare go near you, otherwise, they would kill me. So, I had to stay away for my dear life," he said.

Boma was shocked by what she had just heard, then, she abruptly shook off her stupefaction. The boy might have just been telling a wild story. Why would some people go to beat him up just for giving her a lift? Then she laughed in disbelief.

"You are kidding, right? Why would anybody beat you for helping me?" she asked.

He was serious as he glanced at her. "Yes, they did. They said I must not go near you if I wanted to stay alive. I am ashamed to say that I chickened out for my dear life," he said.

"I still don't get your drift? Why would anyone do that to you?" she asked.

"It was George. The boys were his friends. They are dangerous guys. They beat most boys who ever went close to you," Dele said.

Boma was very surprised. George did not have many friends. He was not the type who moved with a platoon of friends. This story sounded rather out of place to her. However, she began to realise that most of the boys who came to her even after she had broken up with George never came back except one tough guy named Williams. She did not like Williams because he was a known cult guy and he did not hide it. He was also rough.

"Nobody can threaten me to stop coming after you," Williams had told her one day when he had met her on her way to her new apartment. Following her betrayal by Sophia who had gone to bed with George while feigning hatred for him, she had decided that she would not stay with anybody again. Her father too did not want her to be corrupted by the girls in her hostel; he decided to get an apartment for her where she stayed alone, off-campus.

"It is not about anybody threatening you. I am just not interested in having a boyfriend. I am in school to learn and I would appreciate it if you let me be," she had yelled at him and walked away.

Two days later, he had been stabbed badly and hospitalized. She had thought he was involved in one of his many ignoble fights but now, if what Dele was saying was anything to go by, there was more to that fight. Was he attacked?

"George cannot do that," she said.

"Yes, he did. He may be every girl's sweetheart being a fine boy with money but he is also very dangerous and a chief in his fold," Dele said. She understood what he meant and she was further stupefied. She had never imagined that George was a cult boy. She had not seen Williams for almost a year. She was sure she could get the truth from him. If George was truly what Dele said he was, then, the boy must have done a very good job at pouring dust into her eyes because he had her fooled all along

Anyway, George had left the school even though he still came around as if he had no other life away from the university. She had completely shut him out and he, for reasons she did not understand, had refused to give up on her. Meanwhile, he was the reason why she would not give her heart to any boy. Well, Richard! She shook her head.

She might have almost given her heart to Richard but he was not for her. He was not different from George, if not worse.

She sat back and let her mind run wild. Dele was still talking but certainly, she was no longer listening. Barbara was a prisoner of emotion or love for Richard. She had not been any different from Barbara even though hers was mere fantasy. She would have to break away from it. Richard was no good. He was a heartbreaker who would ultimately leave her hurting in the end. What was the need? What was the essence?

I don't love you, Richard. I cannot and will not! You are no good! she screamed in her head. She jolted out of her short reverie and looked at Dele. He was still driving and she wondered if she had spoken the words. She hoped not. Apparently, from the way he focused on the wheel, he did not hear her.

Suddenly, Dele looked at her. Their eyes met. "Did you hear that?" he asked.

Her heart suddenly began trumping. "Hear what?" she replied, her lips quavering as she stared wild at him.

He kept his face lit with his bright smiles. "That from the first day I set eyes on you, my heart has never stopped beating for you. You excite my heart. Each time I see you, my heart flutters and I always yearn for you."

Her heart froze as she stared straight at him. Dele was a charming guy all right but she was not ready for anyone. Not after George and her bruised head in the skies longing for Richard.

"I know how precious you are and I will do my best possible to treat you as specially as you deserve," Dele said.

"Do we have to walk this path again?" she asked.

"We have never walked this path or any before."

"I knew your intentions before you ran away. You will run away again at the slightest threat."

He heaved a sigh, it was heavy. "I will never run away. I will stand as solidly and bravely as a knight and claim my princess."

She too let out a sigh. She looked at him again. Far from it, Dele was nothing near the man she could fall in love with. She could not place what was wrong but he just did not appeal to her in any way. He could at best be her friend and nothing more.

CHAPTER 8

It had been over two months since the day Dele told Boma of his feelings for her. She had not given him a definitive answer and he had taken it that she was biding her time. He also assumed that if he remained patient, loving and caring, she might just one day cave in to him. Though he endured the suspense, he was determined to wait because he was desperate to win her heart. Now, he was no longer as fearful as he was back then when George and his friends frightened him. He too now belonged to an association of friends. Though he was not a strong man in the fold, at least, he was protected.

Dele spent most of his time in the last two months with Boma and they were growing closer and their bond getting tighter. He knew that in a matter of time, he would be officially dating her. Friends on both sides already thought they were dating and took their denial as mere cover.

"What are you doing today?" Boma asked him that Friday morning.

He thought and could not think of anything he would be doing. “What else if not to come by later and be with you,” he said.

She smiled and gave him a loving stare. That always melted his heart. “That is so sweet,” she said.

“A beautiful girl deserves all the attention,” he said.

She nodded. “I see. Anyway, why I asked is because I feel like going to a club tonight to party,” she said.

He looked at her. He was both surprised and amused because he had never thought of her as being that adventurous. He was happy to take her out. “You really want to go to a club?” he asked.

“Yes. Will you take me to one?” she said.

He smiled and told her he would be happy to.

She was pleased. She had been thinking lately that she needed to start enjoying her life again. Since after George, she had been withdrawn and had never visited a club. She had hoped to revive her social life. Dele was now the closest boy to her in school and she thought if he was willing, she could go with him. She wanted to go with a male company so as not to be mistaken for a girl who went to clubs to seek patrons. She just wanted to dance and have clean fun.

She saw how pleased Dele was to accept. She knew that he would be delighted to take her anywhere she wanted because of what he felt for her. He could do anything for her. Were they not always like that? Men! A man would profess love to a woman he wanted and he would demonstrate that love in deeds but when he had got her, he would leave her wondering where all the love went.

She didn't think of Dele as a bad guy. He had been so good to her and had spent most of his free time with her. He always came with something for her even though she was not the type who was impressed by gifts. She liked him so much but that was as far as it could go. She did not think she loved him.

She was seeing Dele off later that morning when a car stopped in front of them. It was a luxury car and she did not need anyone to tell her it was George. George came out abruptly and came towards them.

"Boma! What is this?" George demanded. He was obviously referring to Dele.

Boma held Dele's upper arm and pulled him along but George grabbed her arm. He pulled her back. "I am talking to you!" he bellowed.

"Don't pull a lady that way," Dele said, facing him. He looked angry.

George smirked. "How dare you! You stay out of this! I am talking to my girlfriend," he said.

"Who is your girlfriend? And who are you?" Boma asked, disgusted by the way George had pulled her. Her arm hurt.

"I am George, your boyfriend, the man you are made for and the only one for you forever," George said.

She stared at him, amused. She looked at Dele who was calm and looking at George coolly. "In case you are in a dream, wake up, please. I am nothing to you and you are nothing to me. We have nothing together. I have told you this before; you are a past that shouldn't have been and you are the forgotten past. Stay there and leave me alone," she said, her voice suddenly rising in anger as she vented.

George laughed. "Don't get it wrong, Boma. I have pleaded with you to forgive me and come back home where you belong. For almost three years I've been begging," he said.

"Which home?" she cut him short. "George or whatever you call yourself: Get it into your head that you are no home for me to return to. I know where my home is and you are not welcomed there," she said. She turned to Dele, "Let's go!"

"Boma," George said, trying to hold her again but Dele pulled her to his other side to avoid George's hold.

"You heard her. Leave her alone, man," Dele said.

"You are playing with fire and you know it," George told him.

"Then you don't know what fire is," Dele said. He put his arm around Boma's shoulder as a sign of confident protection and they walked away.

George stared angrily at them as they walked off. He knew Dele all right. He remembered how he had once frightened him and the boy had run off. Now, he was back simply because he thought that he was out of the school. He shook his head sadly and then in pity for Dele because the boy was invoking his anger and he would surely get it very rough. He entered his car and drove off rather speedily.

It was very early in the morning that Dele returned Boma home. She had insisted that he should take her home because she had had enough of the club. The evening had begun well and she had enjoyed it with Dele by her side. She had danced away the evening, feeling very excited. For her, it was a good way to push away all the bad energies around her head; George especially.

Then, just after midnight, George showed up. She was not sure if he had come there deliberately because he had one way or the other found out that she would be there or that it was just a coincidence. It was likely the latter because he came in company of a tall girl named Cecilia who was a popular girl on campus because she had appeared on a soap commercial on television.

Boma had seen him when he entered the clubhouse and had ignored him but as soon as he noticed her, he left Cecilia and came to her. She was dancing and having fun and did not want to give a care in the world but he began to dance near her and soon glided in between her and Dele, hijacking her from Dele.

She was not into drama and was not ready to create one; so, she danced a few seconds with him and when she saw Dele move to her side, she turned and switched to him. George was not pleased. Cecilia who might have noticed something came on the floor. She was a good dancer.

George was seeking an opportunity to go between Boma and Dele but the girl had put her arms around Dele to prevent it and so they danced very closely. It was so much to George's chagrin. However, Cecilia came up to George and danced with him but his mind was not with her as he kept staring at Boma.

Dele felt a sense of pride, and he felt Boma's accepting him was closer than he could think. He was ready to protect her. They danced for some twenty minutes more before Boma said she wanted to sit for a while.

Dele led her to a seat near the bar and he ordered drinks. She had told him that she would take brandy. Dele shrugged. She was from the Niger-Delta region and it was not uncommon to see the girls drinking liquor.

"That boy wants to annoy me, really," she said as she took the brandy in one mouthful. She swallowed and let out a hard sigh. He gestured for another shot but she stopped him. "One is just okay."

He sipped his whiskey and stared at her reassuringly. "Don't let him bother you," he said.

"Of course not."

Just then, George came up to her. He shoved Dele roughly with his shoulder to make way for him. He completely displaced him.

"Hey, what did you do that for?" Dele asked, pushing him by his shoulder.

George turned and stared daggers at him. "How dare you touch me with your filthy hands?" he bawled at Dele, obviously spoiling for a fight.

"How dare you brush me aside with your filthy body?" Dele hit back, squaring up to him.

George was stunned as he stared at him, then he looked at Boma. "You are trying to be a man because you want to impress her? You know me and what I am capable of doing," he said, the threat bare.

"George Douglas, there is nothing you can do to me," Dele said.

George was furious that the boy had called his full name in an effort to demean him. Boma got up and pulled Dele to another corner, obviously to avoid him. He stared at them, frustrated.

"What is the matter with you? You brought me out here and you are running after your ex who obviously doesn't want you," Cecilia said to him.

He stared at her for almost a full minute. "I love that girl. She is my wife to be," George said.

Cecilia was irritated. "And what am I? Another one of your pastimes?"

"You don't understand, Cecil," he said.

"Shut up! I understand. You told me you wanted me for keeps, so what is this nonsense? You are just a pathetic liar and deceiver," she said. He tried to hold her hand but she poured the whisky in her glass at him and walked out of the club.

George was dazed. He looked around. Some people were staring at him. He was humiliated. He got up and stormed out of the club. On his way, he stopped by Boma and Dele. "Hell is coming for you," he spat and walked out.

CHAPTER 9

Dele was dismayed when he brought up the issue of wanting a relationship with Boma and she told him without mincing words, once again, that she was not interested in dating anyone.

"I am happy that we are friends and that is fine. We should not take it any further. If you want more than friendship as we have it now, then, we have better stop being friends because I will not date anybody," she said.

"But you know how I feel about you," he said, frustrated.

"And you know how I feel about how you feel about me."

This was exactly a week after the last time they had gone to the club and she had gone the previous night alone and he had just learnt of it. He had wondered why she did not inform him and she had told him that she just did not want any drama and fortunately, she went to a small club where George did not show up and where she had the time of her life without any drama. Now, he thought differently that she had deliberately gone alone because she did not want him around her anymore. He even suspected that she might have gone with a man she was possibly dating and hiding.

Dele was heartbroken as he entertained the suspicious thoughts. "I have been there for you, ready to face the tempest for you. I truly love you, Boma," he said.

She shook her head. "We've been through this before. I told you I don't want to date anybody in this school and I am keeping to myself."

"Why? Is it because of what George did to you? That was a long time ago. George is not a good person and he is not worthy to have a girl like you. You made a mistake with George, that doesn't mean every other guy is another George. I am not George."

She had tried to make him understand that she could not date any boy but she did not know how else to convince him. Of course she knew her reason did not sound concrete enough but she was not going to date him. She did not like him enough. Deep inside, she knew the only reason she could not date him was that he had run away when George had threatened him as he had confessed. That made him weak. His recent bravery did not extinguish the fact that he ran away. More so, she had vowed that she would not date another man in the school. She was sure if George and his cult friends threatened him again, he would run again for his dear life. Maybe she was just searching for excuses in her head. She just would not take their friendship to the next level.

Dele was too hurt and even angry to hear anymore. He just walked away, his heart in many pieces. He had just fooled himself all along, he thought to himself. He wished he had given up on her from the first day she had turned him down. He had kept a bright hope that actually took him nowhere with her. The hope dimmed and he felt wasted and spent.

Dele's hurt was terrible. He could not sleep well for days and he stayed awake far into the nights worrying and thinking about her and wishing things were different. Why had he fooled himself? He was bitter with even himself. Boma had injured him deep in his heart and he knew that it would be tough to go on. He had always hoped that one day he would truly be the proud boyfriend of the most beautiful girl he had seen. His friends admired him because of her. They were of the conviction that he was dating her, even though he had always played safe by being truthful that they were just friends. However, he savoured the admiration he got. Now, he knew that would transform to mockery.

He always woke up with the thought of Boma on his mind and he would quickly wash up and dress up. Then he would go to her neighbourhood and loiter around in the hope that she would see him and he would act indifferently towards her. He wanted her to see that he was not suffering after all and that he was fine. The truth, however, was that he was suffering and he wanted to see her. He avoided going to her house but he stuck around. Unfortunately, she never came out and he never knew if she ever saw him. Then, he would go around her class. He knew her lecture timetable and he would hover around. Once he saw her walking out of the hall, he would walk ahead of her, hoping that she would see him and call him.

Of course, the first time, she saw him and she did as he had expected. She asked him why he had not come around her and he was acting cold to her and responding through his nostrils.

"I don't want to waste my time chasing shadows."

She exhaled noisily, a signal that his response did not go down well with her. She ignored it. "But you are my friend and you should not be acting like a child, simply because I ruled out the possibility of dating. I just don't want you trying in vain."

"So what is the point? I better keep to myself and let you go on with your life. I cannot be living a lie. People think I am your boyfriend and that is what I wanted," he said.

She nodded intensely as if she was rocking her body. "I see! Anyway, what people think is nothing to me. I like our friendship and I respect that."

He sneered. "Is that why you called me? I have better things to do," he said. He knew he had acted childish the moment he made the utterance but he wanted her to rethink and possibly reverse her stance.

Boma felt disrespected by his utterance. She drooped. "I am sorry to have bothered you. Please, go attend to the better things."

He strutted away, greeting anyone he saw on the way who he knew even vaguely. He wanted her to see that she did not bring him down. She watched him as he walked off. She shook her head because somehow, she understood what he was trying to do and that made his effort a very bad case. She was disgusted.

Afterwards, she ignored him each time she saw him. Every time she came out of her lecture hall, she would see him walk past and it did not take a few times for her to realise that it was not mere coincidence.

Then, he went a step further by trying to date a girl in her class. The girl's name was Benibo. She was a pretty girl and she was friendly with Boma. As soon as Dele began talking to her, she suspected that he wanted to cheat on Boma. She too thought the two had something going. She told Boma of it in her attempt to be a good friend even though they were not so close.

"That is nice. If you like him, date him. He is actually a good guy and he is caring," Boma told her.

"Aren't you two together again?" Benibo asked.

Boma smiled. "We were never together. We are just friends and nothing more. He is a kind hearted human being," she said.

"But he is a cult guy, I don't want to have anything with any boy in any campus confraternity," Benibo said.

Boma was shocked. "No, he is not. Dele is clean," she said.

Benibo shook her head. "Then you don't know him. He is a cult boy and it is not a secret," she said. She called her friend, Hannah, to confirm what she had said.

Boma was shocked. Dele was the same person who had revealed that George was a cult boy and now, she was knocked for six to hear the same being said of him. It was hard to believe. For days, she went about frozen, wondering how he had hidden that from her. In the days that followed, she began to hear more about him. Then, Benibo had called her one evening to a bar where Dele was with some boys. They were drinking and smoking.

"That is the guy whom you said is a kind-hearted human being. Look at the people with him," Benibo said. "Those are his confraternity members and they are terrible people."

Boma was shocked beyond her wits. She did not know that Dele smoked. She and Benibo left to avoid being seen. She was glad she had maintained her stance not to date him because he had been a facade as far as she was concerned.

His farcical character would have fooled her just like George's had.

CHAPTER 10

Benibo rejected Dele and that crushed him even more. However, he did not give up. He went for another girl in Boma's class. The girl whose name was Tari was aware that he had asked Benibo out. She told Benibo and Boma got to hear. It became apparent that he was trying hard to make Boma jealous that he was with another girl. Unfortunately for him, Boma was more amused and felt sad for him. His act to her was sheer puerile inanity.

He did not get Tari either and he went on to another, this time, it was Sophia who was touted as an easy target. She was easy for him all right and he flaunted her. He was always coming to the class whenever he knew Boma was in class and he would try to be sweet to Sophia. Sophia knew of his closeness with Boma but she was a girl far too gone to care about anything. She and Boma had severed ties long ago after George's silly confession. She had moved on and had had many flings. She did not mind that she was gossiped as the most passed-around girl on campus. All she was after was the money and the fun. She had become a happy-go-lucky girl.

One Friday, Boma was in class just after her lecture was over. Dele who had left an on-going lecture in his class was there to see Sophia and he was as usual, overtly expressing love to her. Many times, he would look over his shoulder to see if Boma was looking at him and each time, he got heartbroken that she was busy with other things.

Boma had put Dele and his antics aside and while he continued to try hard at it, she completely ignored him and he did not matter anymore. She just did not care about him. She had been repulsed by his pettiness and now, she just did not give a hoot.

Just as she got up to leave the class, George entered. He looked very handsome and dapper. He was dressed in a three piece suit. He smiled at her. She had not expected to see him around during school hours especially after he had finally graduated from the school. He walked up to her.

Everyone's attention in the class was held by George's surprised appearance. Since Boma was already set to leave, she got up and walked towards the door. Just as she walked past him, he held her arm.

"Boma, please, don't walk away, my love," he said.

She snapped her arm out of his grip in annoyance. He quickly let go of her but he stood in her way.

"Boma, I know you are mad at me all this time for being stupid. I messed up big time and I am forever ashamed of what I did against you," he said on top of his voice so everyone could hear.

Boma was embarrassed. She made to walk off but he prevented her by blocking her again. "I am only human and I know that forgiveness is possible. You are a beautiful creature; I know that fact. You are beautiful inside and out, an angel, so celestial and cherubic. Please, forgive me that my troubled life would find peace and joy from within," he said.

Boma was speechless; her embarrassment paralysing her. She wished the ground would open and swallow her. She stared at him wide-eyed.

"Please, everyone," George said, calling on the class. "I love Boma Horsfall. My life has not been the same since she walked out on me. She gave me the best moments of my life but I was foolish to mess up. I realise my stupidity and I've repented. I want her back in my life. Please, join me to beg her for forgiveness."

Boma was stupefied. What was this devious guy trying to do? She would not let him blackmail her emotionally. She looked around the class. Some boys were already up and coming forward. A few girls rose and were advancing as well.

Dele was staring, his heart beating very fast. Sophia was saying something to him but he was not listening. There was worry all over his face. His heart beat was so fast that it was almost choking him.

Boma watched as her classmates walked up to them. They knelt down and began to plead with her to forgive George.

"Won't you go and beg also?" Sophia said as she hit Dele on his shoulder. He looked at her and grimaced. He looked away. He wished there was something he could do to stop what was happening in front of him. He would not be able to stand it if Boma reconciled with George. Then, like he had always suspected, he reasoned that Boma still carried a torch for George that was why his unfaithfulness had dealt her a painful blow, so hard that she had decided to alter her normal life to move on. She would accept him, especially with the strategy George was using. He wished he had thought of it and had used it instead of trying to get involved with other girls just to spite her and make her feel jealous. It was now that he realised that all that he had done had been in vain because they did not get to her.

All Boma wanted was to disappear from that scene. To her, it was dreadful and she did not want to stand it. Her classmates were begging her and George too was on his knees. He was still talking but she was no longer listening. She was annoyed, in fact, angry with him for putting her in this situation.

"It is okay," she said. "I forgive you."

Most of her classmates cheered. George rose with the others. He beamed that his two-hundred-watts smile that had once held her captive. That smile that now reflected deceit and lies to her; it represented them as well. "Thank you, Boma. You will never regret this," he said and hugged her.

She was already regretting it. She extricated herself from his embrace and made to walk out of the class but he held her arm. "Boma, please, just give me a moment. I want you to know that I am very serious about this," he said. He dipped his hand in his pocket and brought out a small box. The class wowed and some actually clapped.

Boma's heart fell even deeper to depths unknown. What was this? She was both astounded and dismayed. She was wailing her emotional agony in her head.

George opened the box and brought out a bright silver ring. He knelt again and took her hand. The sight of the shining white ornament suddenly captured her. She imagined that the ring was very expensive. He wanted to slip such an expensive ring on her finger as a proposal for marriage.

Dele suddenly rose to his feet but remained transfixed. It was a torture for him to be witnessing what was happening. He felt crushed. He wanted to walk away but somehow, he wanted to see how things would unfold. He hoped that Boma would reject George but a better part of him told him that it was the one thing she had always truly wanted, to have this kind of commitment from George. He wished he could shout it to her that she would only get herself entrapped because a cheater would always be a cheater. George only wanted to be a married cheater. Marrying her was no guarantee that he would change. It would be a disaster if Boma agreed.

"Boma, I love you like I have never loved anyone before. You mean everything to me. I don't have a happy life without you. I promise to be a loving man and to love you for as long as I live," George said.

Her eyes fell on his face. She heaved a sigh. She realised that he truly loved her. He had demonstrated it in all the time he had been begging for her forgiveness. She believed that now that she realised it. She heaved a sigh.

"I have come today to both beg for your forgiveness and go further to beg you to be my wife. Boma, will you marry me?" he proposed.

Many thoughts were running through her mind. She looked up and her eyes met with Dele's. He was staring at her intently. She looked away and looked around the class. Everyone was staring at her, waiting for her reaction. This was George who had given her great moments in the early days of her time as an undergraduate. He was her first love and the six months they had been together had been the most adventurous and greatest moments of her life. Then, she thought of his many bad habits. He was a chronicle skirt-chaser. Yes, she had caught him red-handed with Tombra and she had seen him with many other girls. Even while she was happily in love with him, he had frolicked with Sophia and many others still. She sighed again. People change!

"Say yes," some girls in the class urged her like they would share in whatever the outcome was.

"I am still a student. I came to school to learn and get a degree, not to get a husband. This is not for me at this stage," she said and withdrew her arm. She did not let him recover from the disappointment before she hastily walked out of the class.

She almost ran as she left the faculty. When she got to the park where she would take the cab to the main gates, she realised that she had tears in her eyes. George wanted to trap her and she would never let him do that. She did not love him anymore and he was now a past she dreaded and would never return to.

There was a car horn behind her when she got to the park. She did not turn because she thought it was George. The car horn blared again, yet she did not turn. She just wanted to get away.

"Boma!" she heard her name. This voice sounded differently. She thought she had heard the voice before but she could not place it. She turned and saw the car pulling off the road. She wondered who he was. Then, suddenly, he emerged from the car. Her heart began to pump rather heavily. She was having just too much for a day! She felt her head go light and she feared she was losing consciousness. Perhaps, it was just a dream. It could not be real.

CHAPTER 11

Impelled by some forces beyond both her control and understanding, Boma walked towards him. Her heart was still beating very fast. She was staring straight at him and wondering if this was real. She had just escaped from George trying to propose to her and all she had wanted a moment ago was to be safely in her apartment away from the madness around her.

"Richard?" she mumbled as she got to him. She was still in disbelief. He was staring and smiling at her. His smile gleamed like a million stars around her and it came with an unfathomable effect on her.

"Boma. Yes, it's me and I am here to see you," he said.

"Me? Why?" she muttered almost to herself.

"I am in Port Harcourt for two weeks and your mum asked if I could check on you while I am in town."

Boma could not put a rein on her emotions. She suddenly felt a rush of excitement in her. He had come to find her and he would be spending two weeks in town. However, she controlled her body; at least she had the power to do that. “Good afternoon.”

“How are you?” he said and extended a formal hand to her.

She tried to hide the fact that she sighed. She would have expected him to spread his arms and hug her. She took his hand and shook it. He had the softest hand she had ever held. “I am fine. Welcome.”

“So, where are you going?” he asked.

“I am going to my hostel. I stay off-campus.”

He nodded slightly. “Why don’t you get in the car and we go somewhere and have dinner? Then, I’ll take you home to your hostel,” he said.

Without thinking, she nodded and went around the car. He entered the car, leaned to the other side and stretched his arm to open the door for her. She slipped in and they drove off.

Dele had left the classroom almost immediately after Boma had. Sophia asked him where he was off to but he waved a nonchalant hand at her and hurried away. He knew Boma would be running to her hostel. Perhaps, he could meet her on her way and offer her a ride to her hostel. He saw her just as she got to the carpark and his heart fell to the floor of his stomach when he saw her talking to a strange man. The man was unbelievably handsome and he could see that Boma was captivated by him. His heart broke painfully when she entered the car and went off.

Who was that man? Dele wondered. *Was he someone she was meeting for the first time? Why did she just fall so quickly and go with him?*

He would have suspected that there was a man in her life—her reason for telling him off—but then, that handshake was too formal for people who were close. Whichever the case was, Dele was devastated that Boma went off with him.

Dele was not the only one who had seen Boma enter the car. A boy named Jack had seen her, too. He was a very loyal boy to George and had always looked out for his interest, even though, covertly, since they belonged to the same fold.

George was very sad that his plans to get Boma had failed. He felt so tired and weary. As he dragged himself out of the hall, a feeling of humiliation and embarrassment blurred his vision. He had barely entered his car.

"I just saw Boma entering a man's car," Jack blurted out, running up to him.

George's heart was further broken. He almost lost his voice because, when he opened his mouth to speak, the words were almost without sound. "What man?" he asked.

"I don't know him but he is a dashing young man, devilishly handsome," Jack said.

George was confused. He knew Boma was adventurous, she liked to party and have fun to the fullest but that was as far as it went. She was not wild or wayward. So, what man's car could she have entered?

"Where did they go?" George asked.

"Out of school, I believe," Jack said.

George assumed that the destination would be Boma's house off campus. He had also wondered how she got such a posh apartment and one that was so tastefully furnished at that. He knew that her father was not a pauper but he doubted that her father could have rented such a place for her. Perhaps, she had a secret man somewhere and the man was responsible for her comfort in school. Perhaps, he was also the reason why she was not accepting him again.

George drove to her house. She was not there. He wondered where she had gone. He was dismayed and his heart was shaking. Where could she have gone with that unknown man? It was only then that he wondered what Jack meant by devilishly handsome.

***

Boma kept stealing surreptitious glances of Richard as they had late lunch. It did not seem like it was real. She was itching to have a conversation with him but she did not know how to start. He seemed too engrossed in his meal that he barely looked at her. Was he really like this or was he just trying to be offish with her?

Her eyes were on him when he suddenly raised his head and he caught her eyes. She was slightly embarrassed and quickly averted her face and feigned to get busy with her meal.

"So, how is school and everything generally?" he asked. She returned her gaze on him and she could see genuine concern in his eyes.

"Fine," she said automatically. Of course, with all that had happened that day, everything could not have been fine. Then, she told herself that things might just turn around only because he showed up and it was a big surprise, one she would never had dreamt of.

"And I believe study is going on just fine too," he said.

She nodded. She was thinking of what he had said earlier when she met him at the park. He had come to find her. Did he really come to her school to find her? "What are you really doing here in Port Harcourt?" she asked. This was the opportunity to keep the conversation going.

He beamed at her and she almost choked on her breath. “I told you earlier, I came to find you.”

She smirked dismissively even though she was pleased to hear that. “Get serious, Richard. Why would you come to find me?”

He guffawed. “You don’t believe me?”

She shook her head. “I know you are kidding,” she said, trying to sound dismissive.

With the smile still gleaming on his handsome face, he said, “Anyway, I am on leave and I thought I should come here and spend time. But of course, something brought me here and it is something special.”

A twinge of disappointment hit her. He wasn’t there to find her after all. “What is the something?” she asked.

He heaved a sigh. “Let’s say I will tell you before I leave town. Enjoy your meal, Boma,” he said as he returned to his meal as well.

“Hi Boma,” Tombra said as Boma and Richard walked out of the restaurant. Tombra was with a middle-aged man. She seemed excited to see Boma and that kind of bewildered her because she did not even think that Tombra knew her well.

“Hello,” Boma said, coldly.

Tombra was sizing Richard up and her face was alit with a bright smile that was clearly beguiling. "Handsome dude you have here," she said. She greeted Richard and he responded warmly. Tombra had already graduated from the school but, like George, she still came around and that was simply because she lived in the town.

Boma did not say another word to her and Tombra seemed to understand. The man she had come with was standing patiently and smiling rather foolishly. Tombra turned to him and told him that he should go in as she would join him shortly. Obediently, the man went inside the restaurant.

"Boma, can I see you for just a minute?" Tombra asked.

Boma was not interested in seeing her. "Well, as you can see, I am with somebody. Maybe some other time," she said.

"Just spare me this one minute, please," Tombra said.

"Boma, go ahead and see her. I will wait for you in the car," Richard said.

Boma drooped. It was not something she wanted. She turned to Tombra and stoned her with a tough look. "What is the matter?"

"Boma," Tombra began, "I know it is possible that you are mad at me because of George. George and I never dated. You know how carefree I am. George and I are too alike to have dated. I am not in for dating in school. I am after cash and George is the big player on campus. I was having a good time with him, that's all."

Boma wondered how that was so important to her that she had to talk to her about it. "It is of no importance to me," she said.

"But you broke up with George after that day."

"It is still not important to me," Boma maintained.

"I am not saying you were wrong to break up with him because, of course, he was cheating on you big time. I don't do boyfriends or relationships. I just have a good time and I move on. I am talking to you about me because I don't want you to have any hard feelings towards me. I didn't set out to hurt you."

Boma sighed. "I am just wondering how this is important to me. Truly, it is not. I barely know you or remember what you are talking about. Please, the past is in the past, I don't want it exhumed because I am not interested."

She excused herself and walked off to Richard's car. She was disgusted that Tombra had to stop her to talk about George and herself. As far as she was concerned, they belonged to a past she was never willing to revisit.

CHAPTER 12

What's your tomorrow like?" Richard asked as soon as he pulled up in front of Boma's apartment.

She did not lend it a thought before she answered, "Nothing much. I only have one lecture and it ends by ten."

"May I come around to pick you up from here by ten thirty then?" he asked.

She almost gushed out a positive response but she was able to get hold of herself. "Pick me up to go where? I thought you came to town for something special," she said.

She was quiet for a moment; she remained seated in the car, obviously waiting for him to say more. He raised his eyes and deliberately let them sparkle as he drew a smile. She almost gasped each time he beamed that smile.

"If you don't want me to pick you up, then it's fine," he said.

"No, that is not what I mean. Of course, I will be delighted to go out," she said rather earnestly, afraid that he had sensed that she was turning him down. "It's just that I don't want you to miss your purpose of being in town."

His smile was brighter. He looked happy. "Don't worry about why I am in town. I will come here tomorrow at ten," he said.

She nodded. Somehow, she felt bullied but she somewhat liked it.

Boma's legs wobbled as she walked into her apartment. It still felt like a dream. Richard was here with her and he wanted to see her again tomorrow. She felt a sense of insufferable elation. She threw her bag on the couch and hurried to the window to peep out. He was driving away and she watched his car until it disappeared from view down the road. *Oh! Richard! If this is a dream, I better not wake up.* She realised that she was grinning to herself. She felt so light and it was as if she had wings and could fly.

***

Richard lay awake far into the night. He was thinking about Boma; that cherubic child of love and sweetness, the ravishing beauty that had held his heart captive from the first day he had set eyes on her. He never forgot that day; he had gone to visit Patrick and was with him outside the house when she arrived. It was a few days before Christmas. He had held his breath! She was a perfect beauty. Her beauty radiated like a million stars that brightened every crevice of his heart and life amidst clouds of all his despair. He had never felt love like this before. It was immediate, so sudden and at first sight. So, his friend's sister was this breathtakingly beautiful and he was just meeting her.

He knew Tonye from secondary school days. She was the most beautiful junior girl he had ever seen and he had wished she was his mate. He could not have anything to do with Tonye, of course, because she was too young, plus, she was Patrick's sister. At that stage in life, it was against the rules of boys' friendship to date a friend's sister. It was an unwritten rule of solidarity. It was worse because Patrick saw him as a spoilt boy who was always wooing girls just to dump them. He recalled that Patrick had once labelled him as an unrepentant Casanova. It was a joke but underneath it was a true reflection of what Patrick actually thought of him.

As they grew, he always thought of Tonye and when she visited Patrick once at university, he had been fascinated at her beauty because she had bloomed into a beautiful late teenager.

"You are a stunner, Tonye," he had said to her.

Patrick had frowned at him and told him not to pay such compliments to his sister. "What do you mean she is a stunner? That she is stunning you or what? I don't like it.

Don't tell my sister that," he had said; his disapproval strong and written all over him.

"It is just a harmless compliment. You know that your sister is drop-dead beautiful and her beauty shines like a thousand watt electric bulb that can illuminate even the darkest corner of a man's heart," he had said, smiling. Tonye had been flattered but her brother was angry.

"Richard, leave my sister alone. Don't ever dream it that you can have anything to do with her. You know that I know you, and I do not permit you coming near my sister. The day you will do it, you would have crossed the line," Patrick had said. He had not been mincing his words and Richard, though embarrassed, had decided not to upset his friend.

He had endured Tonye's beauty and in later years when he had come across her, he had just remained cool with her, relating with her like a sister. The feelings had naturally faded off with time and he and her related just fine. He could now pay her compliments even in her brother's presence, especially now that he knew that she had a serious relationship with a young military boy.

However, when he met Boma, everything in him including his very essence longed for her. She was exquisitely beautiful with a rare touch of undiluted innocence. She exemplified a darling baby. It was heartfelt love at first notice.

Patrick had noticed his enthralment and had frowned at it. "Boma is my kid sister and I will do everything to protect her from you. I disapprove that you should even like her," he had told him shortly after Boma had gone inside the house.

"Why are you always against me admiring your sisters?" Richard had asked.

Patrick had shot him a solemn look that knotted his face. "I don't want you to admire my sisters. Listen, Richard, I've taken you like my brother and we have come a long way. Please, stay off my sisters, don't admire them. Just keep off them. If you cannot take them as your sisters, then don't notice their existence," he had said.

"Why are you talking like this, Patrick?" he had asked his friend. "You should be happy that your sisters are beautiful and men like me find them fascinating."

Patrick had frowned deeper. "Men like you should not find my sisters fascinating. Listen, I am warning you. It won't be funny if you dare cross the line. Friendship comes with boundaries, when you desire my sister, you have crossed the borderline. So, please, don't cross the line. It will pack up whatever relationship we have," he had said. Then he had exhaled hard. "Guy, you have Barbara, face her and make the best of your relationship with her."

Richard had been bruised. So, he would have to forfeit this beautiful girl he was very sure he had fallen in love with?

This was the first time he felt this strongly for a girl yet he was forbidden to have anything to do with her. He valued his friendship with Patrick who had brought him home and he had grown close to his family, even Tonye was now more like a sister to him.

Then, he thought of Barbara. She was a very beautiful girl and she was kind and generous. He had liked her like he had always liked beautiful girls. Barbara came with something extra, though—sophistication. He had first met her with Patrick. They were close and his friend had told him that she was his former colleague.

"She's exotically beautiful," he had told Patrick. He meant the compliment.

Patrick had thrown a haul-over-the-coals look. "Look at your silly mouth, 'She's exotically beautiful,'" he had mimicked him. "Is it every beautiful girl you must admire?"

Patrick had told him not to channel his energies towards her because it would not work. "She is up above your league. She is not a girl for small boys like you," he had said. Obviously, Patrick had been trying to discourage him. He had let it pass and taken his mind off her.

The next time he would meet Patrick, his friend had told him that Barbara had been asking after him.

"What for?" he had asked, actually surprised that she had asked about him.

"She is foolish enough to fall for your good looks. I feel obliged to tell her that behind the good looks is a merciless and brutal viper but I am only restrained because you are my friend," he had said.

Richard had frowned. "What do you mean I am a merciless viper? Listen, Patrick, I may have been a bad guy but people change as they grow older. Why can't you understand that I have changed? I am not getting any younger. I should be thinking of a serious future," he had said.

Patrick had laughed hysterically and he had wondered what was funny. "Can a leopard change his spots? You can tell anyone this cock-and-bull story but certainly not me because I know you. You leave havoc in your trail."

He had told him that he would be different this time. He meant it. Patrick had been reluctant. However, Barbara found her way to him and they became very close. He liked everything about her. He had been determined to keep her and possibly marry her but Barbara had a dark side. There was somebody in the mix and she was hiding the person from him. He found out and that hurt him. She was seeing a big politician who was doling big money to her. It was then he realised that she had been living far above her means. He felt cheated. He was ashamed of himself and could not yet tell Patrick about it because he felt Patrick would laugh at him and say he had met his karma. He talked to her about it but she denied, claiming that the politician was her relative. It was a foolish claim as far as he was concerned. How could a politician from the middle belt be related to her when she was from the far south?

Barbara had pleaded with him and assured him that she loved him and would never do anything to hurt him, but she was always travelling to Abuja for one thing or the other under the pretext of business; business that had no nature. He was convinced that she was doing something terrible and which she found hard to detach from. At that point, the only thing he wanted was to break up with her but he felt trapped because he had wanted to prove to Patrick and those who thought he was unrepentantly wayward that he had changed. Then, it was worse because Barbara was gloating over him. It was like they were inevitably heading for the altar, but for him, the altar were the rocks.

The day he met Boma, he felt instantly emotionally re-engineered, and that instant, Barbara diminished and he knew that the rocks were closer than even he had imagined and hitting the rocks could not be avoided. But then, Boma was forbidden, her brother had expressly, and seriously so, told him to steer off his sister. He had tried to stay off and it hurt him so badly. He still struggled with the feelings. Now, he was at a crossroad, to chase Boma and win her heart and damn the consequences or to painfully put her behind him to save his friendship with her brother who had been almost a life-long friend. He sighed. He would take his chances however dangerous they were.

He knew when he had an effect on a girl. He had always known that and that moment he set his eyes on Boma, he noticed that she reciprocated his fascinations. The enthralment was mutual and that made him desire her even more. He would surely take his chances. Someday, Patrick would understand, especially when he realised that he had not only truly fallen in love with his sister but he had also respected her by not tampering with her emotions. Time would exonerate him. He was sure of that. He thought of Sopriye! Ah ha! He did not crucify Patrick back then. Patrick had no idea that he knew what had happened yet he had forbidden him from having anything to do with his own sisters.

CHAPTER 13

George was disgusted when he saw Dele in school talking with her early the following morning. He had come to check on her again since he did not see her the previous day and he had been very disturbed to think that she was with another man. He wondered what Dele had come to do there. He was already aware that Dele was seeing Sophia; and Boma no longer had anything to do with him.

"Boma, I know I must have messed up with my behaviour. Forgive me. I want to be your friend again," Dele said.

Boma was surprised that Dele had stopped her just as she was about to enter her class. She threw a disinterested stare at him. "Forgive you for what, Dele? You did not offend me," she said.

Dele shook his head. "I know I did. I did not mean to hurt you," he said.

She was puzzled. "Hurt me? How? You did not hurt me in any way," she said and giggled.

That hurt him. He wilted. "Okay, just forgive me that I was dating someone else in your face."

She shrugged. "How is that an offence? You should date whoever you want that accepts you."

That was a heavy blow to his heart and it shattered it. It just meant that she truly did not feel a thing for him. How could he be gallivanting in an effort to get her jealous and she did not even notice? How foolish she was making him look.

"Can I be your friend again?" he asked.

She gave him a cool stare. "I have been having the greatest moments of my life lately and I am fine."

Dele's heart missed a beat and began beating fast. She was enjoying her life without him. "Could it be that man who came to pick you up yesterday?"

She grimaced as she stoned him with an irritated look. "There's something I don't really like about you. You should learn to always mind your business. Please, excuse me," she said and walked into the lecture hall.

Dele felt his head spin and it was as if he was blanking out. It broke his heart even more to accept that Boma had not changed her mind about him. What could he possibly do to make her accept him?

Just then, George walked up to him and stared him straight in the eyes. "You just won't give up and leave my girl alone, will you?" he asked.

Dele hissed and walked away. George smiled. It was time to teach this boy a bitter lesson. He wished he was still a student; it would have been easier for him to mobilize his squad against the boy. Even at that, he still had people on campus he could talk to. Dele needed to be dealt with and severely.

Boma left school as soon as her lecture was over at ten. She needed to get to her hostel, take a shower, dress, and wait for Richard. She was anxious to see him again. She had barely slept the previous night as she had several disruptive dreams of him and her being together in moments that were their very own fracturing her sleep.

She was dismayed when she got home. George was waiting outside. Her heart fell. *What is the meaning of all this?* she thought in annoyance. She stormed towards the house, demanding what he was doing there.

"Boma, I need to talk to you. You humiliated me yesterday when you walked out on me after turning down my proposal," he said.

She stared angrily at him. "Listen, George, or whatever you call yourself: I am not interested in your proposal and I have told you to keep off. What don't you understand when I said you should leave me alone?" she barked.

"Love never gives up. True love is persistent," he said. "I love you truly."

"I am sorry, George. I don't love you and I don't want you; and just in case you are in any doubt, be sure that I will never and can never love you. So, go away," she said, her anger unabated.

"I cannot leave you, Boma, I can never stop loving you."

"Then, good luck to you. Please, leave!"

He stared at her for a long moment, his chest heaving hard. She made to walk into her apartment but he stood in her way.

"I will never leave. You must accept me again; otherwise, I will go nowhere."

Boma was shocked at his words. A sudden fear assailed her. What did he mean he would go nowhere? She did not want Richard to meet him there. She did not want Richard to know him and she did not want him to meet Richard. She relented as she looked at him.

"George, please, go home. You graduated from school almost two years ago. Go on with your life. There is someone out there for you," she said.

He smirked. "There is nobody anywhere for me. You are the only one for me and that is why you must accept me back."

She shook her head. She was frustrated. She thought that she could go in and lock the door and get dressed, then go outside to wait for Richard. But what if George forced his way in with her and got into her house? He could do anything to her. The greatest fear that tugged at her heart was him raping her. What could she do to make him go away?

She decided that she would just leave in the hope that he too would leave. She turned and began to walk away but he went after her and grabbed her by her arm.

"You are going nowhere. We will settle this matter right here," he said.

That instant, she knew that she was in trouble and that was the moment she deeply regretted the day she met him. She tried to wriggle her hand out of his grip but he held firmer.

"Let go of me. You are hurting me!"

"Then, listen to me and take me back!"

"You cannot force me. Love cannot be forced. Leave me alone!" she screamed. She began to struggle with him.

Just then, some neighbours overheard the noise and came out. They demanded to know what was going on.

"This man here is harassing me."

"I am not harassing her," George countered. "She is my fiancée."

"Who is your fiancée? Let go of me," she yelled at him.

"Leave her arm," a tall boy said. He came forward and tried to separate them.

"I don't want her to leave," George said.

"Just leave me alone!" she screamed. The other neighbours told him to let go of her.

Now, George realised that the neighbours, especially the boys, there could soon get angry that he was holding on to her against her wish and they might attack him. He released her.

She stared angrily at him. "Now, get out of here and don't you ever come here again," she barked, livid with anger. Tears were now burning her cheeks. She felt harassed by George.

Just then, from the corner of her eyes, she saw Richard's car driving in. Her heart dropped. This was the scene she never wanted him to meet. She stared angrily at George and that instant; she frantically struggled with the urge to jump on him and attempt to sink her nails into his throat and strangle him. Then, a new fear hit her. What if George tried to attack Richard? It was more than probable that jealousy could spur him to act irrationally?

“My brother is here now. Misbehave and he will deal with you,” she suddenly said. Naturally, George would show respect for her brother, she assumed. George turned to look at the car. He instantly looked waned.

CHAPTER 14

Richard did not take Boma to any fanciful restaurant as she might have expected. He took her to a house that was tastefully furnished. She was confused and wondered what he was up to, albeit she stayed quiet. However, she fervently hoped he was not about to attempt anything funny.

"This is where I stay when I am in town. It actually belongs to my cousin who is out of the country," he said.

She looked around the place. They were in the living room. "Nice place," she remarked. She remained on alert.

"Feel free and at home," he said, flashing his usual radiant smile at her.

She nodded but did not sit. She was staring at him. He raised a brow as he looked at her again.

"What's the matter?"

Her lovely eyes shot at him like the arrows from an archer's bow. "Why did you bring me to a home? I thought you wanted to take me out," she said, emphasising the last word.

He let out a hard sigh. He cast his stare on her and she reciprocated the look. They locked stares for a long moment. He took a step towards her and impulsively, she moved two steps backwards. He paused but continued to fix his stare on her.

"Why did you bring me here?" she asked.

"It's because I want to be with you, talk with you alone in our own space."

Her heart was beating too fast. She could not decide if it was dread or excitement, but the pulsation was heavy, thumping. "Our space?" she asked.

He sighed again and she thought if sighing was second nature to him. "Boma, please, sit down. I want you to trust me. I won't do anything stupid," he said.

Her mind went to Belema who was her roommate in her first year. She had gone to visit a male friend she had a crush on, on his invitation and to his house. Belema had returned that night, shattered because the guy had violated her. That had hurt Belema to her soul because after that day, she became a shadow of herself. Though the young man was arrested because one of the girls in the room who heard Belema's story had gone to report the case to the police and the guy was sent to prison upon conviction, Belema's life had remained scarred and traumatized. Was this what Richard had in mind? She began to think of what she had in her bag that could be a weapon. A nail filer! She held her bag close to her.

She remained standing.

"Boma, trust me. I am a friend of your family; your brother is my best friend. I won't do anything to hurt you."

She walked to a couch and sat very gingerly, her eyes on him, her heart almost bursting out of her chest. He looked so handsome like a black prince drawn out of a fairy tale, so perfect, so captivating, and so attractive. Her heart would always beat for him but she was so scared of being defiled even by a man who held her so enthralled.

Richard went into the kitchen and shortly afterwards returned with fried chicken and chips with fruit juice. He served her.

"So, tell me. Why exactly did you bring me here?" she asked; an attempt to loosen up.

He sat on a couch opposite her. "I want to talk to you. Yesterday, I told you I came to town to find you," he said.

"Yes, and that is because my mum told you to check on me."

He guffawed. “I apologize for that. Your mum doesn’t even know I am in Port Harcourt.”

She grimaced; disappointed that he had lied to her. “So, why did you say that?”

“But I later told you something brought me here and it is something special,” he said.

“Yes, I remember that but that doesn’t answer my question of why you lied that my mum said you should check on me.”

He was silent for a moment. He had his eyes still fixed on her and she wondered if he did not think that could cause her some discomfiture. “Boma, the truth is that I came here to find you and be with you. That was the first thing I told you yesterday when you asked. I told that innocent lie because I did not want you too startled.”

She was quiet and staring at him. When he paused, it was obvious that her silence meant she wanted to hear more.

“You see, I have always been a bad guy. I play with women’s emotions. I make them fall in love with me and I run away afterwards,” he said.

She was dejected to hear that confession; it was horrible even though she knew he was telling the truth she already knew. She wondered why he was telling her about that horrible part of him. She remained quiet. His eyes fell on the tray he had placed in front of her. She had not touched it.

“Have your meal,” he said.

“I am listening to you,” she said flatly.

“I always thought I was loveless, that I could not love a woman truly and be with her for long. I was wayward and emotionally irresponsible. Patrick used to jokingly call me an emotional criminal. I have been loved by the most beautiful ladies but I had hardly cared. Dating was just a kind of sport for me. Then, last year, I made up my mind to change and be responsible. It had been something I had always wanted to be, have a focus relationship-wise,” he explained.

Boma listened on, her mind ticking like a clock. What was her business with what he was saying? She was not sure it was something she wanted to hear but she still found herself wanting to hear more about him. Her brother had been right; Richard was not a serious person when it came to dating. She questioned herself why she was always excited about him.

“But everything for me changed that day I set eyes on you. You took my heart and ever since, I have never stopped thinking of you. I thought I had seen the most beautiful of ladies but when I saw you, I was sure you are the masterpiece of creation, you’re so beautiful, so angelic; you just encompass everything that means beauty at its best," he said.

It was a struggle for her as she heard those words pour out of his mouth. She struggled not to smile, not to expose the fact that she was flattered and elated by the words. Her eyes dropped as her sight hit the floor. It was an obvious attempt not to look into his eyes because she was sure he would see her emotions in hers. She steeled herself. Her brother had told her that Richard had a sugar-coated tongue and he knew how to pay compliment to a girl the same way he knew how to break the same girl's heart. What made her own any different? He was doing the same, trying to mesmerise her so that she would fall for him and he would teach her another devastating lesson why she must never let down her guards when it came to love and loving. He was, from what she had heard, the monster of love; unfortunately, good and adept at crushing and shattering hearts.

She kept her face averted this time, staring at the pack of juice but actually not seeing it. Her eyes were in her mind, watching the turbulence his words were stirring in her.

"I know it is hard to believe but I have never been this truthful. I longed to see you every day but I could not. I was forbidden to have anything with you. I was in pains and it hurt me to layers deep in my heart. You filled my mind and all I wanted to see was you," he said.

“I don’t understand what you’re saying,” she muttered, almost voiceless. “Forbidden how?”

“Your brother does not want me to have anything to do with you. I knew it would kill me to see you, as angelic as you are and endure your superlative beauty. So, I stayed away but I was suffering. You see, the day you were returning to school, I showed up only because I wanted to see you. I had learnt that Patrick was dropping you off at the airport and I came around. I so much wanted to go with you to the airport but then, your brother is smart,” he said.

Where was Barbara in this mix? Boma knew Barbara existed prominently when he met her. So, where was she in all this time? “Richard, maybe we should talk about something else. This talk is making me uncomfortable and I really don’t know where it is going,” she said. She looked at him, hoping frantically that he would not accept her request.

His eyes dimmed, sheer disappointment and a worse feeling settled upon him. This time, his sigh was noisy. “I’m sorry if I upset you. You are the only reason why I came to Port Harcourt, the special reason and that is because my world is dark and gloomy without you. Your beauty alone brightens the darkest corners of my life. Since yesterday, I have been the happiest man only because I am here with you,” he said.

She was still struggling with herself. She was getting overwhelmed by the feelings that he loved her and wanted to be with her. It was the same way she felt but she could not let him know that because he was Richard, the dangerous heart breaker. “I am happy to see you too, after all, you are my brother’s friend and I appreciate your care,” she whimpered, breathing a bit faster than usual.

“Boma, I love you. I know it will cost me my friendship with your brother but I am willing to let go of everything just to win your love. You are my treasure and I want to cherish you for the rest of my life,” he said.

She stared at him, speechless. A surge of happiness roused in her. Somewhere deep in her heart, against all what she knew of him, she believed him. He loved her and would love her forever. This reputed and famed heartbreaker loved her truly.

CHAPTER 15

Richard had just dropped Boma at her house later that day. He wore a solemn look, apparently weighed down because he had not got a definite response from her.

"Whatever you do, just know that I love you more than anything that ever lived or will ever live. I will never stop loving you even if it would cost me my very essence. Not to love you is sacrilege for me," he said just before she got out of the car.

She smiled at him for the first time. "You are an amazing guy, so sweet and great. Thank you for everything," she said. "I will look forward to see you within the next twenty-four hours."

"I could come and take you out tonight," he said suddenly excited.

She shook her head, her face still lit with the smile. "Go home, Richard. Not today. Goodnight," she said, and practically ran away to avoid hearing his next word. She imagined excessive happiness pumping in her heart and circulating through her veins. She went to the bathroom for a few minutes and when she returned to the window to watch him, she was surprised that he had gone.

She fell on her bed, exhausted by the excitement in her heart. Richard had professed love to her! He loved her!

Just then, a knock came at her door. She jumped up. *Is it Richard?* she thought.

She went to the window and peered through. His car was not there but she could see the body of a man by her door. The knock came again. She could not see the face. Who was it?

She went to the door and peeped through the hole. It was Jones, one of her neighbours who had been around that morning when George had tried to harass her. He was the particular boy who told George to leave her. What did he want? Why was he at her door?

She opened the door and slipped out. She never allowed boys into her apartment. She would rather come out to meet them.

"Good evening," she said to him, her face creased by an enquiring grimace.

"I had checked on you earlier. Something happened near school today. George was stabbed and was rushed to the hospital," he said.

She was shocked. She asked what had happened. Somehow, because she knew George, she felt concerned.

"He was involved in a fight with a boy. I understand, it was over a girl. It was a big fight and the other boy knifed him twice. One on his neck and the other in his stomach," Jones said.

Fear seized Boma. "His stomach?" she screamed, alarmed. "He killed George?"

"No, I don't think he's dead but it is critical. I was surprised because he was here this morning disturbing you," Jones said.

Boma was shaking. She thought of George. She fervently prayed in her mind that he was okay. She did not wish him dead. She asked Jones if he knew the hospital he was taken to.

"No, I don't but I won't advise you to go there. You are the girl in contention," he said.

Wide-eyed, Boma's jaw dropped. She was stunned that the boys had fought because of her. Instantly, she knew the other boy was Dele. So, Dele had fought George and stabbed him. She did not think Dele was violent or capable of inflicting dangerous injuries on a fellow. She had nothing to do with both of them. She had told Dele that she could not reciprocate his feelings and he seemed to have moved on by dating Sophia, although, only that morning, he had come around her. George was chasing shadows because she was long done with him. Yes, he could not accept her refusal but she too could not entertain his persistence.

However, she was afraid that if George died, she might be beset by a crushing sense of guilt that she was in the middle of the fight that had snatched his life. Her fear was visible all about her. She did not know that tears were already streaming down her face.

That night, she could barely sleep. George was on her mind. How could he have gone to fight with Dele? Or was it Dele who went to fight him? She hoped that George was responding to treatment and that he would survive. She prayed for his survival.

The following morning, Boma went to find George at the university teaching hospital. She suspected he could be there. She was not wrong. There were many people just outside the gates and they were talking about the incident.

"Why would George get into a dangerous fight over a girl?" she heard.

She was able to locate his ward but she could not see him because he was actually in the intensive care unit. She felt so depressed that George was in there, fighting for his life.

Why had he not just given up and forgotten about her and gone away. He would not have been in this situation. Then, Dele! She wanted to get angry with him but restrained because she did not know what had really happened. It would be unpardonable if Dele was the aggressor.

Just then, two boys walked up to her. She suspected that they were students. The boys were frowning at her.

"Hey, what are you doing here?" one of them asked.

She stared at them, befuddled. "How does that bother you?"

"You know it's all your fault that George is there battling to live," the other boy said.

She stared outrageous at them as if that thought had not crossed her mind before. "What do you mean? I wasn't even there when the fight happened. I only learnt of it last night," she said. She already guessed that the boys were George's friends. She did not know them but they knew her.

"We all know you are George's girlfriend but you dumped him because of that boy, Dele. George has never stopped loving you; he never wanted to give you up because he loved you sincerely. Now, your boyfriend is not happy that George doesn't want to give up on you. He stopped George and asked him why he was still coming around school yesterday. He came prepared because he started a fight almost immediately and stabbed George with a dagger.

Once he did that, he ran away but, of course, he won't run for too long because there is no hiding place for him under the sun," the first boy said. He had dark eyes that held meanness so naturally and it did not require much brain wracking to surmise his wicked capabilities.

Boma closed her eyes in her desperate effort to control the upheaval in her mind. It was for a brief moment. When she opened them, she looked tough at the boys. "Now, listen, George was a fling, we did not last more than six months. He was into other girls and I let him be. We were finished and we needed to be on different lanes as it should be expected. Secondly, I did not dump him. He cheated and I quitted. Thirdly, Dele is not my boyfriend and has never been. We were friends at some point and when I did not accept to take it beyond the friend zone, he walked off and began to associate with some girls. So, tell me, do any of them have any claim over me that they should fight? If they fought, it must be because of something else, not because of me," she said.

"Something else like what?" the first boy asked.

"Personal grudges," she answered.

"Boma Horsfall, your story is rather very convenient. We all know what has been going on. You shut George out because of Dele. Just pray that George lives, otherwise, hell will prevail," the first boys said, his voice cold and piercing that for an instant, it sent a tremor through the girl.

She was irritated as she stoned him with an angry look. "What is wrong with you?" she asked in frustration. "Anyway, why am I even having this discussion with people I don't even know," she said and stormed off, walking away from the ICU. She had to get away. Then, it hit her that the boy had called her name in full, an indication that he knew her very well. She thought of what Dele had told her about George being a strongman in a campus confraternity. Those boys were definitely his members.

She hurried out of the teaching hospital, tears welled up in her and threatening to fly out. She went to school and to her department. She noticed that people were staring at her as she walked. She felt really terrible. Once she entered the hall where her course-mates usually stayed while waiting for lectures, the class went quiet and everybody in the class seemed to turn to look at her. She walked to her regular seat and sat, mortified. The tears that she had been struggling with finally cascaded down her face. She was overwhelmed by emotions. She wished she had never in her life met George and Dele.

Sophia came to her and sat beside her. She put a hand around her. Boma was terrified because she and Sophia had stopped being friends after George's confession that he had slept with her while she was her friend and he was dating her. What was the Judas up to? To deal her another kiss of betrayal? She stared at her amidst her watery eyes.

"You just have to be strong. It is not your fault, honestly. I mean you are a very beautiful girl and men are easily attracted to you. George and Dele went too far with this and now George is in critical condition. Had George gone on with his life after graduation, this would not have happened," Sophia said.

It was now it occurred to Boma that Sophia had had a thing with the two boys. She stared at her, wary that the girl was up to something. She dried her eyes with a handkerchief from her handbag.

"You just have to be strong and don't let this matter weigh you down. It is unfortunate it happened but it is not your fault," she said.

Boma did not say a word. She just stared at her former friend. Fortunately, a lecturer walked into the class. Sophia returned to her seat at the back. Boma's mind was in turmoil. She honestly wished she had nothing to do with any of them.

CHAPTER 16

Richard was waiting in front of her house when she returned to the hostel. He looked at her quizzically. She looked weighed down by some troubling thoughts. He spread his arms to hug her and was glad that she fell into his embrace.

"Boma, what is the matter? You look troubled," he asked. "Did someone offend you at school?"

She exhaled hard. "Welcome, Richard," she said. She knew there was no way she could hide it since it was all written all over her. "You met some people here yesterday morning. I don't know if you noticed the guy who left in a car as soon as you came."

"Yes, the fair complexioned guy. He seemed very angry."

She was surprised that he noticed that and wondered why he did not mention anything about it yesterday even though she spent almost the whole day with him. She nodded.

"What about him?" he asked.

"He got stabbed in a fight yesterday and he is in critical condition at the teaching hospital," she said. "He is Ambassador Douglas' son."

Richard raised his right brow. "The former minister?"

"Yes. He got into a fight with another boy and he got badly stabbed."

Richard sighed and she noted it. He was always sighing. "Okay, what really happened?"

She opened her apartment and ushered him in. She asked him what he cared for. He said he was okay. He asked her again what had caused the fight. Boma told him everything. Richard felt a pang of jealousy that she had dated George and he was her first love. He wondered why George could be so stupid to cheat on such a beautiful girl and lose her. However, he was glad somewhere deep in his heart because her breaking up with him had only made her available to him. Then when he heard about Dele and how close he had been to her and why she had refused to date him because of George's betrayal that had caused her to swear against dating, he had his new fears. He may be swathed by the same response. He was, however, glad that she did not accept Dele and the many boys who had come her way.

Despite himself, he did not blame George for not giving up on her. Boma was irresistibly beautiful and certainly too precious to lose. Even at that, he still thought that George ought to have still let go of her and forgotten all about her. He was also pleased that Boma did not hold on to George like most girls would have because of whose son he was. This was the kind of girl he had always dreamt of; one who loved only because of love.

He smiled at her after listening attentively to her. “You have no fault in it. The young men were foolish. Real men don’t fight. They both don’t deserve you,” he said before realising that he sounded selfish. He looked at her for her reaction. She was staring at him, astonished.

“If you had a chance to have me as your girlfriend, would you fight for me when some man threatens to take me away or you will just walk away?”

He gasped for breath for a moment as his heart shook. She had trapped him. He forced a smile that did not fool her. “Well, my feelings for you are stronger than any other resolve. I know that fighting is wrong but not when it involves a superlatively beautiful woman like you, I will not hesitate to go to war if any man tried to steal you from me,” he said.

Just then, there was a knock at her door. They exchanged glances. She asked who it was.

“Open the door, it’s the police,” a male voice shouted.

She was surprised. Why would the police come to her house? She opened the door and a uniformed policeman with two plainclothes was there. He called her by her full name and when she answered, the policeman told her that they had come to invite her to the station.

"What for?" she asked. She already suspected that it had to do with the fight.

"In connection to a dangerous fight yesterday," one of the plainclothes said.

Richard heard the policemen and he came to the door behind Boma.

The policemen exchanged glances with one another. "You must be Mr. Dele Peters," one of the officers said.

Richard was shocked. "No, I'm not. And I don't know why you are inviting her to the station over a matter she knows nothing about."

The lead policeman smirked. "You will follow us too to the station for proper identification."

"Are you arresting me as well?" Richard asked.

"No, we are not arresting anybody. We are just inviting her to the station to write a statement of what she knows concerning the fight and for your proper identification since you denied that you are not Dele Peters," the policeman said.

"I have an ID to show who I am."

"You will be asked that at the station. Shall we?" the uniformed officer said.

At the station, Ambassador Douglas was there in the Divisional Police Officer's office with his wife, and some people who had come with him were outside the station. One of the plainclothes led Richard and Boma to the DPO's office.

"This is the lady, sir, Boma Horsfall. And we found this young man in her house," the officer reported to the DPO. "We suspect he is Dele Peters."

Ambassador Douglas rose swiftly and angrily; his big frame gave him an intimating disposition. He grabbed Richard by his jugulars. "So you are the scum who stabbed my son!" he bellowed and violently shook Richard.

"He is not Dele!" Boma shouted, offended that the man had rough-handled Richard.

The huge man stared embarrassed at Richard, his grip loosening. "You are not Dele?"

Richard was too stunned by the man's attack to even speak; he shook his head.

"Then, where is he?" George's father asked.

"I don't know him," Richard stuttered, trying to regain his composure. He knew Ambassador Douglas very well as he was a public figure being a prominent politician. He was, however, disappointed that the man had physically attacked him without even being sure of who he was. It was even worse because he would have inflicted injuries if he was truly Dele yet the man as a former ambassador was a diplomat who ought to know how to exercise decorum.

"Who are you, mister?" the DPO asked Richard in a tough voice that was unapologetic and commanding. He was a tall man with weather beaten face that told tales of his many gruelling years probably as a junior officer in bad situations.

Richard produced his ID card and threw it at the DPO's table, a sign that he was very angry with what had happened. The DPO examined the identity card and let out breath from his lungs. "You work in Lagos. So what are you doing here in Port Harcourt?" the top police officer asked.

"I am from this part of the country. I am currently on leave and I came to see my fiancée only for your men to come to her house and bring us here," Richard said.

The DPO looked at Boma. Despite herself, Boma smiled. She was pleased to hear Richard refer to her as his fiancée. That somewhat doused the tension in her current predicament.

"How many boyfriends and fiancées do you have?" he asked her.

Boma's smile instantly transformed to a tough frown. "I beg your pardon, sir! What do you mean by that?"

George's mother was quiet. She was just staring at Boma. Boma had noticed and had deliberately ignored her.

"You are aware that the two men George Douglas and Dele Peters are your boyfriends and they had a dangerous fight over you," the police officer said.

"No, they are not my boyfriends. George took advantage of my naivety in my first year to date him but that did not last long because he was chasing everything in skirts. We broke up since then. Dele is just a friend who wanted more but I turned him down and he moved on to date another girl in the department," Boma explained.

"But people who are in the know said that the fight was because of you," the police officer said.

"I don't know anything about it and I have nothing with the two men," she said. She seemed to have some sort of confidence and she figured it was because Richard was there. Now, she noticed also that George's father was staring at her. He seemed captivated.

"But you are a beautiful lady, why didn't you amicably resolve your issue with my son?" Ambassador Douglas asked.

Boma shook his head. "He cheated on me; it broke my heart and I got done with him. To be fair to him, he apologized but he never changed and I was not cut out for that," she said.

A heavy sigh escaped from George's mother. She was a very pretty woman with a bright light skin that had obviously been maintained with sophisticated cosmetics. She shook her head slightly but said nothing. Boma imagined that the woman would hate her for being the reason why George was in the hospital.

"You will write a statement," the DPO told Boma.

"No, she is clearly not at fault in any way," George's father said. Boma was surprised. The man who seemed very angry a moment ago and was almost ready to asphyxiate Richard was the one exculpating her.

"That is true. She is innocent," his wife added. She had a strong voice and it was the first give-away that she was possibly the one who called the shots at home.

The DPO rose and shrugged. "Okay, if you say so," he said, resignedly.

"We are sorry to have bothered you," George's mother said. "You are such a beautiful young lady. My son is such a fool to lose you. Please, find it in your heart to forgive him." It was a regrettable voice that came from her. George's parents had walked them off out of the station.

"I have forgiven him, ma. Long ago," Boma said.

"No, you have not," the woman said. "If you have truly forgiven him, you would have been back with him. I liked you the moment you walked into the DPO's office."

Boma's eyes shifted to look at Richard. George's father was talking with Richard. The man had his arm around Richard. She knew he was apologizing for his earlier attack. Then, George's father extended his hand and they shook hands. That moment, Boma thought that George was fortunate to have such good people as his parents. However, she did not want to encourage the woman because she understood what she meant.

"It's nice meeting you, ma," Boma said.

"Yes, same here. I wished I knew when you and my son were dating. I would not have allowed him to misbehave, but one thing I am sure of is that George has changed. Don't allow any man to come between you and your first love," she said.

Boma experienced sheer discomfort and she kept her face away. The woman seemed to understand. She held her hand and squeezed gently. "It is fine. I am sure you and I can be good friends."

CHAPTER 17

Ten days had gone by since Richard arrived in town. He was with Boma every day and he was in his best elements, doing everything to make her both comfortable and happy. He so much occupied her that the issue of George and Dele became distant to her. She learnt that George pulled through and was responding to treatment but she did not bother to visit him. She did not want to create any false intention.

"Boma, I have told you I love you and I want to remind you that I still love you," Richard said. He had just returned her to her hostel and they were still in his car. A country song by Don Williams was playing from the stereo. She kept her face away from him. Even at that moment, she wondered why she had not accepted him. She had not rejected him either; she just had not given him a definite answer yet. She wondered if he knew that she loved him.

"I notice that you are always playing country music. You remind me so much of my father. He plays country music every morning while he prepares for work," she said. It was true. Country music was what always played in her family house because of her father. Funny enough, she had never had any serious interest in country music. She hardly knew the songs though she could recognise some songs and the singers. She knew Don Williams, Tom Jones, Kenny Rogers, and Dolly Parton as they were her father's favourites. But Richard was always playing Don Williams.

"I think I am a peaceful person and country music is for peace and serenity," he said.

She smiled as a fatuous joke came to her head. She almost said, 'peaceful heartbreaker,' but she stifled the urge. It came as an amused smile.

"So, let's talk about us. What will you do with my feelings for you? I am for real. I will never leave you. I will always love you and be with you for the rest of my life."

Hesitantly, she looked at him. "Do you know what it means to be real? Like being completely truthful?"

"I have been truthful with you. My love for you is pure and real and will forever remain constant."

"Then, why did you not tell me about Barbara?"

He was silent for a moment that seemed like eternity. "What about Barbara?" he finally asked, rather solemnly.

"You know who Barbara is, don't you?" she asked.

He sighed and nodded. “Yes, I do. She’s my last girlfriend who is your brother’s close friend. She and I did not work out.”

“Or you meant to say you dumped her as you normally do?”

“We did not work out,” he insisted.

“So, why did you not mention her in all our discussions?”

“I told you I have dated many ladies, the most beautiful ladies but I never mentioned any name or talked about any specifically.”

She turned away. She was sure that her brother was right about Richard. He was a heartbreaker who never cared about the ladies he dated. She feared she was just another of his target but she had some impulsion to believe him and that even baffled her. She could not understand it. “So, you see me as your next in line to use and dump?” she asked, her face returned to his to catch whatever emotion she could get.

His face did not betray any emotion. He kept it solemn. “I see you as my first true love, the one I want to spend the rest of my life with,” he said.

She laughed impulsively. “I am sure you felt the same when you met all the beautiful ladies you boast to have dated,” she said, wondering why she was getting quite petulant.

“I am not boasting. I am ashamed of myself for those exploits. I am making my life right now.”

“You must have also said these same words to Barbara.”

His sigh followed. “Boma, can we just concentrate on us and forget what I have done?”

“What you have done are determinants of what you will do,” she said. She was beginning to enjoy the tease; she was being frisky but he did not seem to be having any of it and she just wanted to continue.

“Not in this case. A repentant man knows what he mustn’t go back to,” he said.

She laughed at him. “Richard, I am not a kid and I am sure you know that. I know what you want,” she teased on.

He wilted out of frustration. “What I want is to love you forever, Boma.”

“That is what men will always say. Maybe the truth is just, ‘I want to love you for the moment, enjoy myself and when I meet the next pretty girl, I’m done and I will move on.’ Forever ends there.”

He adjusted on his seat and turned midway to look at her. “Do you really know what love is? I mean, have you experienced what love is?” he asked.

The queries seemed to drain the repartee off her. She was silent for a moment, obviously chewing over his questions. "Yes, I have an idea of what love is. And yes, I have been loved before. George loved me and he still does. I just lost my vibes for him," she said, reflectively.

He stared straight at her. "I have no business coming to Port Harcourt. You are the only reason and motivation why I am here. If I did not love you, it would not ever occur to me to come down here. If I wanted something else, I would not leave Lagos for it," he said.

She snorted as if she disbelieved him and that cracked his heart. "So, you just want to love me forever?" she asked.

He shook his head. "No!" he said. He had his eyes boring into hers, as if he was searching through the recesses of her soul. "I want you to love me forever as well. True love is requited," he said.

She was quiet again, pondering on his words. She assumed that he was intelligent and somewhere deep in her, it scared her. "Richard, I am sure that you also know that love does not rush and that a girl needs her time in matters like this. I don't want to be rushed into falling in love."

She expected a sigh from him but he disappointed her. He reached for the volume control of the stereo. Another of Don Williams' song was playing. He increased the volume.

"Don't think about tomorrow,
It don't matter anymore,

We can turn the key
And lock the world outside the door."

Then he joined to mime the lyrics. "*I need you so now, come on let's go now. Kick off your shoes, turn out the light, and love me tonight."* His eyes darted to her but the stare was cool. He continued miming. *"Now don't you worry, we're alone now. Let your hair down. Sit by my side. Turn off the TV, put on some music. Pull down the shade, turn out the light and love me tonight.*"

She was suddenly annoyed. "Are you ignoring me to sing?"

He turned off the stereo and faced her. "I am sorry. I should be leaving now. Goodnight," he said.

She was shocked. Was he angry? She stepped out of the car. She bent over the window as she slammed the door. "Goodnight Richard," she said.

He only nodded. He put on the stereo again and without another word to her, he reversed the car and drove off. She stared at him with a falling heart that threatened to shatter. She suspected that he was angry. But why? Had she said something she was not supposed to have said? She took very weak yet heavy steps towards her apartment. Her head was light.

Just as she got into her apartment, she thought he was just trying to make her feel bad that she had not accepted him, despite all that he had said. She was relieved that it was just his game plan. He would come the following day like he always did and she would reprimand him for the way he left her tonight and so abruptly.

The following day was a Saturday and Boma was up early. She had thought that instead of going out that day, she would suggest that they stayed in her place so she could cook and they could talk and see some movies that she had. She hurried to the market to get some things to make lunch.

By noon, Richard had not shown up. She was sure he would come. He always came to see her. She prepared *Jollof* rice and fried chicken dipped in spicy tomato sauce. She was set to receive him. She dozed off on her couch while waiting for his arrival. When she jolted out of her short sleep and looked at the time, it was three in the afternoon. What had happened? Why was Richard not here yet?

When it was five, she became worried and sad that he had not shown up. She began to fear that he was annoyed with her and had probably left her since she was not forthcoming. He must have noticed that she too was so much into him and must have wondered what was stopping her. She missed him, and by nightfall, she was a complete wreck of emotions.

By the evening of Sunday and he had not come to see her, she was sure he was never coming for her again. She was so unhappy and wished that she had not resisted him so much. She loved him and wanted him as much as he claimed he wanted her. She was so restless and she resolved that she would go and find him the next day.

That night, her neighbour was listening to Don Williams and the song filtered into her apartment. It was the same song that was playing over Richard's car stereo that Friday night and it made her miss him so much and her heart longed for him. She would go to him and apologize and tell him she was ready to take the risk to love him. Even if he was a heart breaker, she felt too powerless to stop herself from loving him. She could hear his voice as he mimed those lines and his voice in her head was more distinct than the one that flowed from her neighbour's apartment.

Sleep eluded her as she was deep in thought all through that night and could not sleep until in the wee hours of Monday. She had two classes that day but she was not sure she would make it to any of them. Richard was too much in her thoughts.

Boma found her way to Richard's cousin's house where he was staying very early in the morning and once she got there and saw that his car was not there, she knew he was not at home. However, she went on to ring the bell at the door. There was no response. She became more worried as she feared that he might have left for Lagos.

She looked around for the neighbours but there was nobody in sight and she was reluctant to go knocking on people's doors. She felt a debilitating sense of loss. She regretted that she had not acted seriously with him that night and now, this was the result. He was gone! It broke her heart.

Boma waddled out of the compound, thinking about Richard. He must have been really hurt and angry with her that night that he had stayed away and even left without seeing her. She suddenly felt exhausted and washed-out. She got to the road; and the road suddenly looked long and endless. The thought of the seemingly long road to her house came with a dread not to even attempt.

She stood by the road side, waiting for a taxi. She was very sad.

A car slowed down in front of her. It was a big luxury car. The car passed her and stopped, then, it began to reverse, obviously to meet her. She was irritated. It was a normal situation that men usually pull over whenever she was on the road looking for a taxi. They would offer her a ride of which she never accepted. Her father had expressly told her never to accept rides from people she did not know no matter how much they insisted and she had always done that. She hissed as she threw her face away when the car finally stopped in front of her.

She began to walk away from that spot, a clear indication that she did not want any ride from anybody. She was too sore by Richard's action to leave without telling her after keeping away for two days.

"Boma," she heard a female voice call from the car.

She wondered who it was as she turned to look. A pretty matronly face peered out of the back seat window. Boma recognised the beautiful face and bright light complexion. She drooped and apologetically began to walk back to the car. She greeted the woman.

CHAPTER 18

Richard was worried as he left Boma's department. Nobody had seen her that day even though she had lectures that morning. She did not show up. He had returned to her hostel but she was still not there. Where could she have gone? He decided to wait in front of her house in his car. She did not show up and it was obvious she was not home. A neighbour had said she had seen Boma leaving the house very early and believed the girl went to school.

After a two-hour wait, Richard decided to return home. He wondered what was happening. Was she angry with him for staying away? Or she had simply pushed him behind her and moved on. This girl was difficult, he thought. No girl had resisted him and he wondered why Boma was proving so tough. Perhaps, her brother must have told her so much about him and she was being careful. Obviously, from what she said the last time, she had some information about him. He was no longer the man he used to be. He was now a changed man who had fallen helplessly in love and with her. So, why was she trying to be his nemesis by hurting him with her resistance?

He had stayed away to give her the chance to miss him if she ever would, but now, it seemed to have gone wrong. She was not home and she was not in school. Where could she then be? Then a consolatory thought hit him. Could she have gone to look for him at his place because she was worried that she had not seen him? He doubted it but he still hoped so. He decided to hurry home. If she was not there, then, he would be sure that she had put him behind her and gone on with her life.

He got to his cousin's house and she was not there. He was heartbroken. In that instant, he regretted that he had given her the space to miss him. It had only backfired and he would be leaving town tomorrow. He may never have the chance to win her. He was sure that not winning her heart would torment him for a very long time if not for the rest of his life. He slumped into a couch. He felt so enervated.

***

George's mother was happy when she saw Boma that morning and had urged her to get in the car, promising that she would drop her anywhere she was going. Out of sheer courteousness, Boma had entered the car.

"My daughter, how are you?" she asked, smiling gaily at Boma.

"I'm fine, thank you, ma," Boma replied. She was too drained by her predicament to offer a sincere smile.

The woman noticed but she feigned she did not. "I haven't seen or heard from you after that day. Or are you angry with us for the summon to the police station?" she asked.

"No, ma, I am not angry. I have just been busy with school."

"George left intensive care unit some days ago. He's recuperating just fine in the ward," the woman said.

Boma nodded, wishing she could smile but her troubled mind would not permit.

George's mother seemed to notice that the girl was not interested in talking about her son. She changed the topic. "Do you live here in Port Harcourt?" she asked.

Boma kept her face straight, hoping she was not doing anything the woman would misconstrue as rude. "I am actually from this part but I live in Lagos. That's where my family is."

"I go to Lagos very often. In fact, we have a house there but I can't actually live somewhere else outside Port Harcourt. I love it here," the woman said.

Boma forced a smile that did not come out well. It looked more like a smirk. "I hear people say that but I like Lagos life," she said.

"You do? Lagos life is not for me. Everything there moves too fast and you never get too sane in that kind of place especially when you are on the road," George's mother said and laughed.

Boma was quiet now. She wanted that quietness and she wished she could have it so she would wonder about what Richard had done to her. She was heartbroken. How many times would Richard break her heart without even dating her?

"Who are your parents, dear?" Boma heard George's mother ask. She looked at the woman, perplexed. The older woman repeated the question.

"My parents are Dr. Tari Horsfall and Mrs. Ibinabo Horsfall," Boma said.

George's mother was pleasantly surprised. Boma saw that she was smiling lovely at her. "Wow! Such a small world! I wasn't wrong when I called you my daughter."

Boma looked at her, wondering what she meant. "I don't understand, ma."

The woman laughed. "I know your parents very well. Your mother, Ibinabo, and I were best friends in secondary school. We both attended Archdeacon Crowther Memorial Girls' School in Elelenwo. Her name then was Ibinabo Harry-Powder."

Boma's jaw dropped. She knew her mother had attended Archdeacon Crowther Memorial and her maiden name was Harry-Powder. She and Tonye used to laugh at the name when they were younger and wondered why anyone should be named Powder. Her mother had told them there was a story behind the name, a story she never told them. George's mother knew her mother so well. She wondered why her mother had never talked about her since she was married to a prominent politician.

"I know your father as well. He's a medical doctor. He schooled in London and when he returned, he went straight to marry your mother. Your mother did not want to because she did not know much about him but her family gave her no chance and today, here you are, the product of their union, the most beautiful angel," George's mother said. "Our family is friends of your family. I attended your parents' wedding and they attended mine too."

Boma's stupefaction made her speechless. She just stared, amazed. Truly, it was such a small world.

The woman seemed very happy at the discovery. She asked Boma where exactly she was headed. Boma decided to go home against going to school. She just wanted to rest her head and maybe cry over her loss. She had lost Richard, she thought.

"Okay, where is home, on campus?" the woman asked.

"I stay off campus, ma—down the road opposite the school," she said.

The woman looked at her and smiled. She placed a hand on her shoulder. "So this beautiful angel is Ibinabo's daughter. I always knew only beautiful things come out of your mother. She has always been a wonderful creature," she said.

Boma took it as a compliment and tendered her appreciation. The woman was still smiling at her.

"I am actually going to see George. Perhaps, the driver will drop me at the hospital, then, he will take you home," George's mother said. "Have you visited him since the incident?"

Boma felt ashamed that she had not, especially now that she knew that the woman knew her parents from way back. "I did the day after the fight but I could not see him because he was in ICU," she said.

Boma noticed that the woman gave her a look that clearly suggested that she did not believe her. Then, the woman smiled rather unctuously. "Oh, that's nice of you," she said. Boma also noticed that the woman was too fond of her not to make her think she disbelieved her.

"I honestly went there that morning and two of his friends were there. They blamed me, I felt really terrible," Boma said.

The woman suddenly turned empathetic. “Oh! But it wasn’t your fault actually because you did not send them to fight. George is so much in love with you and he is determined to win you back. You know what they say about true love: it conquers all.”

Boma began to fear that the discussion would veer into the dreaded route. She decided to be quiet.

The woman patted her gently on the back of her palm. “There’s power in forgiveness. As humans, we have our shortcomings and we are liable to err but forgiveness heals all hurts and gives us hope for a better, brighter tomorrow.” Boma only nodded but mutely.

It came with huge relief for Boma when the car drove into the university teaching hospital. She looked forward to the woman alighting from the car and she would be on her way home, away from the tactical appeal of George’s mother to accept her son. George was the very last person she wanted back in her life. He was all she dreaded.

The car stopped near a ward and George’s mother made to alight but she hesitated and turned to Boma. “Boma, sweetheart, why don’t you accompany me to the ward to see my son. I won’t stay long. And afterwards, we will drop you at your place so I can go for a meeting at Diobu,” she said.

Boma felt completely sapped. This was what she never wanted but she found herself suddenly obligated to the woman. Without making a suitable decision, she nodded and came out of the car. She clenched and unclenched her fists in silent frustration. She regretted accepting the ride in the first place. She should have told the woman that she was waiting for someone instead of jumping into the car. She scolded herself for not thinking fast and for not anticipating that this could happen. Now, she would go to see George and that would wilfully ignite for him what she had hoped was long over. She wished something could happen that moment that would make her vanish from that spot and find herself anywhere else.

It was that moment that Richard had arrived at her house again and was waiting for her to return from wherever she went. He had waited until it was noon. He left. He was disturbed even more when he got to his house and did not find her there. He became restless. Then, a crazy thought sneaked into his mind. What if Boma had gone to see George at the hospital? What if she had forgiven him and was back with him? What if George's father had reached her and made her the same offer he had made to him that evening as they left the police station.

He should have warned Boma but he had felt it was not necessary to have discussed it with her. It was a man-to-man talk and he had felt he did not have to mention it to her, at least not now. However, he felt crushed and guilty now that he had not told her. If she went back to George, it meant the painful and devastating end of his dreams to have and cherish this beautiful child of light. It would injure him so deeply to depths unknown.

CHAPTER 19

George stared in pleasant disbelief when he saw Boma walk into the ward with his mother. He smiled and his eyes were filled with happiness. He was lying on his sickbed with his head and half of his body popped up.

"Boma," he called.

Boma drew a smile that came with an effort. "Good morning George," she said.

"Good morning Boma. Thank you for coming to see me. I was told you were here to see me the morning after the fight. I am so happy to see you," he said, gleefully, his eyes sparkled with an exhilaration that came from deep within. He looked at his mother and greeted her.

"Boma is a very nice girl. She told me she was here the morning after the fight and you just confirmed it," George's mother said.

"I feel much better this instant as I am seeing her, except if this is a dream," George said.

His mother laughed. "It is no dream, son. Boma is here for real. You won't believe that Boma's parents are my friends. Her mother and I were secondary school best friends."

George was surprised. He turned to Boma, wide-eyed. "Is it true?"

Boma nodded. She was lost for words to say to him. She knew he was having the wrong idea and she did not want to encourage that.

"Boma, sit down," George offered her a seat beside his bed.

She sighed. "Thank you but I am fine. I just came in with your mum to see how you are doing. I hope you're getting better," she said.

"Yes, I am much better, especially now that I am seeing you. When Jack and Edwin told me that you came when I was in ICU, I was very happy and now that I am seeing you, I feel like the happiest and healed man right now," he said and laughed.

His mother too laughed and placed a hand on Boma's shoulder, "Boma, thank you so much for coming and making my son so happy; you mean so much to him and you give him so much joy. Whatever way he has hurt you in the past, please, forgive him."

Boma's discomfiture heightened. Her eyes rose and glanced at George, he was beaming radiantly at her, expecting to hear her respond. She hated this situation and that hatred continued to grow, the regret increasing as well.

"George knows I have nothing against him," Boma said. She was careful because she did not want to give either the boy or his mother any hope.

"Forgiveness ought to be total. You left me because I hurt you, to forgive me means you should come back to me and let us be the way we once were," he said.

She was screaming inside her head, telling herself that she ought not to be there having that conversation and yelling at them for trying to put her in a tight corner. However, she managed to keep the storm in her head away from them. "We have moved on and we have found happiness with other people," she said, calmly.

George shook his head. "No, I haven't found happiness with anybody. I proposed to you not long ago," he said, his voice dry and he swallowed air.

She had to be brutal now, she thought. "You have found happiness with many girls after me. You've been with so many of them."

"They did not represent happiness to me. I never loved them. You are the only one who makes me happy, the only one whom I love and truly so."

Boma shrugged. She had to be ruthless with him if she must escape the pressure George and his mother were about to subject her to. George was not the man she ever wanted to be with again. He was a shameless, puerile heartbreaker and she was certain he was incorrigible. Even if he had changed, he was no longer whom she wanted to be with.

"Well, I have found my happiness elsewhere and I have never known happiness as much as I enjoy it now. It would be perfectly wrong of me to leave or hurt someone who has given me so much happiness," Boma said.

George's eyes dropped as his heart beat increased. "You have someone else!?" he asked, then, his eyes rose again. "It is not true. I found out that you and Dele were only friends and when he tried to ask you out, you turned him down, saying you have sworn off love because I broke your heart. Dele is dating Sophia now," he said, a dint of hope rousing in him.

Boma shrugged and looked at George's mother who suddenly looked forlorn. "It's not Dele. Your mother has met him," she said. She remembered that he too had met Richard. The thought that Richard had left troubled her afresh but she held her comportment.

"It's okay," George's mother said. "Let's not dig up what will hurt but I believe love can never be lost for those who have it so long as there is life."

George just stared at Boma. He was obviously hurt and possibly heartbroken. She felt a swift sense of satisfaction. It seemed like sweet revenge because she thought she had felt worse pain that evening she followed Sophia and Dani to the bar where he was necking with Tombra. She looked at her wristwatch.

“I am sorry, I have to leave now,” she said.

George’s mother did not hesitate. She told George that she would be back after dropping Boma off. She was walking out of the ward with Boma when they ran into George’s father who was just coming in. He was amazed yet glad to see Boma as he recognised her instantly.

It was about a quarter after noon that George’s mother dropped Boma at home. George’s father had not allowed her to leave as he had engaged her in a discussion. His wife told him who Boma’s parents were and the man was flabbergasted. He looked at her closely and said she truly looked like her mother. He was happy to know that she was the daughter of his old friends.

The man talked with her about her father and that detained Boma. George was quiet and just staring at them. His father did not make any reference to him. He just talked about Boma’s father, how he knew him and how their friendship had spanned over thirty years. He said he and her father were jolly good friends. Boma felt better because he did not mention George or make attempt to reconcile her with him. She was grateful even though she harboured a fear that he was waiting for the right time to broach the subject. He did not and she was happy. However, he took much of her time.

So much had happened. She kind of liked George's parents because they showed her love and she began to imagine that she would be happy if she ended up with George. George truly loved her. He had demonstrated that for far too long. He had shown contrition for over two years and had never ceased to beg her for forgiveness. George! She recalled how he had felt when she told him that she had found happiness elsewhere. He was broken! She saw that. His mother too was hurt.

Boma wondered what would happen if they ever found out that she and Richard were not dating and that Richard had left because she had foolishly not given him a definitive answer to what he sought. The sadness that Richard had left town without telling her crept into her head again. If he truly loved her, he would not have left just like that.

Was this not typical of Richard after all? He would just have used her and dumped her. This was early and clear giveaway of what he would have done, she thought. She had not even started dating him and he was already getting angry and even left town—though, he claimed he came because of her—without telling her.

Just then, the voice of Don Williams crooning those lines that had flowed from Richard's car stereo began to sound in her head as if a cord from a detached source was plugged to her head. Her heart melted as she imagined his face. She missed him. Perhaps, she had pushed him to be angry and to leave. A man who came all the way from Lagos because of her and expressed his feelings for her, yet she was beating about the bush, reluctant to accept; though, it was all she wanted.

She shook her head. Was she not getting herself in an emotional crossroad? One minute she was thinking of George and now, the next, it was Richard. She went to her refrigerator to find something to eat. She had not made anything today. There was nothing there she could eat immediately. She finally settled for cereals and milk.

If she dared returned to George, she would regret it, she told herself. George had a dark side. She remembered what Dele had told her about him and what Benibo too had said about George and Dele. They were members of violent campus cults. George was a cult guy and she found that unacceptable. Then Tombra's voice echoed in her head. *I am not saying you were wrong to break up with him because, of course, he was cheating on you big time*. She shook her head.

Then she suddenly fretted when she remembered the last thing George's father had told her as she left the hospital. He had extended an invitation for her to join his family for lunch next Sunday. Her heart jumped and, again, she was screaming in her head, rejecting the invitation she had already accepted out of courtesy.

She missed Richard so much. Shortly after her meal, she dozed off on the couch. She had not slept enough over the night because her mind was in turmoil over Richard's not coming to see her for two days and that had deprived her of meaningful sleep.

CHAPTER 20

The continuous and relentless knocking at the door woke Boma from her sleep. She was startled.

"I am sure she is inside. A big car dropped her a while ago, and she went inside," she could hear Jones' voice. She shuddered. Who was he talking to?

"Boma!" Jones called out.

She hurried to the door. She was still groggy. Just as she opened the door, somnolence deserted her eyes as she saw a disturbed Richard staring at her. She was stunned and she thought she was dreaming on her couch.

"Richard," she mumbled almost inaudibly.

"I was here early in the morning and I was at your department and I returned here and waited till noon," he said.

Her jaw dropped. She was confused. Richard was still in town. He had not left and he had been out looking for her since morning. She still thought she was dreaming on her couch. Jones was standing there beside him, relieved that he had been vindicated about his claim that she was inside.

“I’m sorry, I was out early in the morning and I returned not long ago and slept off on the couch,” she said. She did not want to tell him she had gone looking for him that early morning, especially not in front of Jones.

Richard thanked Jones and the boy left. She ushered him in.

“You had me really worried,” Richard said. He was staring strangely at her as he sat on a couch.

She cleared the empty bowl she had used for her cereals and tidied up the room. She noticed he was still staring at her with those strange eyes. What was he up to? To tell her that he was giving up on her?

“Why are you staring at me like that?” she finally asked.

“I am just wondering what I can do to win your heart, for you to trust me for what I say and believe that I am for real. For you to love me back.”

She wanted to jump on him and tell him she was all his but she restrained herself. “I actually thought you had left,” she said.

His forehead creased. “I came to town because of you. How would I leave without telling you? I am actually billed to leave tomorrow.”

“I went to your place very early this morning and did not find you there. I didn’t see your car and I assumed you had left,” she said.

His eyes widened incredulously. He was not even sure he believed her but he experienced an unbearable sense of elation that she had gone to find him. She must have missed him as he had wanted if it was true that she went to look for him. “I left home early to come here. I was told you left early for school and I went to your department and no one claimed to have seen you.”

“That was because I was out at your place.”

Richard’s head went down a bit. He was thinking about the big car he was told had dropped her off earlier. He wanted to ask but he was afraid not to get her dander up even though he doubted that she would get upset. “I was here till noon,” he said. “I waited.”

She told him what had happened. He listened attentively albeit with a rapidly trumping heart. The fact that it was George and his parents again caused his heart to miss beats. Suddenly, they formed a potent threat he was afraid he could lose her to. However, that explained the big car that dropped her. He wondered why she had allowed them to bring her to her house. Did she not realise that they would know how to access her? Then, he dismissed the thought. George already knew where she stayed. The fact that George's parents were friends of Boma's parents made his heart panic even more.

"So, why did you abandon me?" she asked.

He let out his habitual sigh which she had also noted came whenever he was in a difficult situation or when a question he would rather not answer was posed to him. "You made me feel I was rushing you and I decided to give you space. You said love does not rush and that a girl needs her time in matters like this. And you said you don't want to be rushed into falling in love. I wanted to stay away for a couple of days so you could figure out if you felt anything for me. If you did, you would miss me, if not, you would forget about me," he said.

"Richard!" she said, finally finding her laughter energy. "You are a master in emotional manipulation. Truly, you are."

He refrained from smiling or getting carried away by her exhortation. The matter was more serious than that, he assumed. "I am, however, happy to hear that you went to look for me. There must have been a reason."

She drooped. "Those two days were difficult for me. I was so lonely and missed you so much. I thought you were angry with me that was why I went to find you and it was worse when I didn't see you and I assumed that you had left town."

He suppressed the smile that came from his soul. "I couldn't have been angry with you. I was dying to see you again and it was painful staying away. The days were the longest I have ever spent in my life," he said. "Boma, please, accept me and just trust me. I don't have a reason why you should trust me but I know for sure that I will never take your trust for granted, not for a moment in the rest of my life."

Her heart was pounding and she feared that it might burst out of her chest. She kept her gaze on his face. He was the most dashing young man she had ever seen, her perfect prince charming, and the one who was too good to be true. She had crushed on him the first day she had seen him and she had found herself too weak and even incapable of pushing the thoughts of him out of her mind, despite all that she had heard about him. This moment, she pushed aside all that she heard about him. It did not matter that he was a serial womaniser who caught his fancy in breaking ladies' hearts. All that mattered right now was that he loved her and she loved him too and he wanted her and she wanted him back.

"Richard," she said in a heavily emotional laden voice, yet solemnly, "there will be fights for me ahead. Will you be tough enough to stand and fight?" she asked. She felt it deep in her that he might face turbulent times, especially as she was sure that her brother would not accept him.

"No matter the fight, I will never leave the only girl I truly love."

Her breath came out hard and noisily. "I loved you from the first minute I saw you and I have loved you ever since but you seemed too far away, unreachable," she confessed, her head recalling that moment he threw a quick and insouciant, 'Hi Boma,' at her.

She had never seen such a radiant smile as that which came on his face now. It was so bright his handsome face looked like the sun, so glorious, so happy, and so joyous, and somehow, it looked so magical. It was the sheer happiness that came from the deepest layer of his being. "Boma, that is why I am here, to reach you and be accessible to you, to love you and be loved by you, to have cherished moments we could call our very own; to start the beginning of a wonderful yet blissful life together. I love you, Boma," he said.

She moved towards him and as if impelled by some cupid force, he spread his arms and she fell into his embrace. He cocooned her and she felt warm and safe and she wished she could melt into him, to be a part of him forever. This was her distant dream come true. She felt an exhilaration that only came from the innermost core of her heart, giving her a sense of both satisfaction and completeness. She had won her love and he too had her as his valued trophy.

"That Don William's song you mimed in your car that evening haunted me while you were away. I missed you so much," she said, suddenly afraid that this excitement would end as soon as he left for Lagos tomorrow. How would she survive without him? Then, suddenly, she had a plan.

"What song was that?" he asked, trying to remember it.

"Where we can turn the key and lock the world outside the door," she said.

He muffled his smile as he glared at her. She looked so sweet and so charming. "Oh, ok. I love Don Williams' songs. In fact, I love all country music but right now, one is playing in my head. It is by Kenny Rogers," he said.

"The gambler?" she asked. That was the only Roger's song she knew or could remember.

"No," he said and shook his head gently. "I will sing it from the second stanza." Then, he began to sing. He had a clear dulcet voice with rich notes. "*Like a rhyme with no reason, in an unfinished song. There was no harmony, life meant nothing to me, until you came along. And you brought out the colours. What a gentle surprise. Now, I'm able to see all the things life can be, shining soft in your eyes,*" he crooned, staring deep into her eyes. Her eyes beheld paradise that he wanted to remain there forever. Then, he sang the chorus. "*And you decorated my life; created a world where dreams are apart. And you decorated my life by painting your love all over my heart. You decorated my life.*"

She smiled even broader. He had sung the song so personally that it was apparent that he was saying the words to her. She melted even more and held on to him. Their eyes locked into each other, staring deep into their souls, searching for their essences in each other and seeming to find all the answers their hearts sought, until they felt their lips upon each other and for a lost moment, they were engulfed by the passion and fire that burnt in their hearts.

When she pulled her head back, she stared at him dreamily and she was panting, trying to catch her breath. His lips stretched with a smile of appreciation and the moments were recovered. He knew he had found his home in her heart.

She moved away from him and sat on the couch, a sense of shame blinding her. She kept her face covered in her hands. He came after her and sat close to her.

"May I ask you a question?" he asked.

She nodded, still hiding her face in her palms.

"Did George's father or mother make any offer to you?"

She turned to look at him, puzzled and confused. "How do you mean?"

"Well, I should have told you this since but I wasn't sure if it was necessary. However, I think you should know. The man offered to pay me five million naira if I agreed to walk away from you."

She was shocked. "And what did you do?"

"I told him you were worth more than all the riches of this world to me. I would never do that."

The delight spread in her and she told him she would never betray her love for him so long as he remained true to her. She was thinking about George's father also. Perhaps, this was the opportunity to cut off from him and his family, after all. She was not interested in what they were after. She could never be interested.

The following morning, Richard left Port Harcourt. He stopped by her house on his way out of town and they shared another passionate kiss. Tears streamed down her face as she watched him drive off. She prayed for a safe trip. She wondered why he had driven down instead of travelling by air.

CHAPTER 21

The days that followed after Richard returned to Lagos were the loneliest Boma had ever had. She missed him so much and wished they never had to be apart from each other. Everything reminded her of him. Each time she heard a country song playing, the thoughts of him would flood her mind and she would long to be with him. And it seemed anywhere she went, she always heard someone playing either Don Williams or Kenny Rogers. What was even more painful was that they had no photograph together and she did not have any of his.

George's father sent the driver to pick her up for lunch the following Sunday. She was sure that George had been discharged from the hospital but she had no impulsion of honouring the invitation. She did not want anything that would threaten her love for Richard. The fact that George's father had offered Richard money to leave her was enough justification for her to refuse to honour the invitation. She sent her apology that she would not be able to make it because she was busy at home.

The driver left only to return about an hour and a half later. This time, he did not return alone. The man who had sent him was seated at the backseat of the big car. The driver came to her apartment and told her that his boss wanted to see her.

Boma was shocked that Ambassador Douglas had come down by himself to her house. She became jittery. She went out to meet him, already thinking of what to tell him.

George's father smiled at her. He did not look offended as she had feared. He asked how she was doing. Then he asked her why she had refused to honour his invitation, despite the fact that he had extended the invitation days ago and she had accepted.

"I am sorry, sir. I have school assignments to finish because I am submitting it tomorrow morning," she said. She hoped he could not see through her lies.

"Oh, I see. But you see, nobody turns down my invitation. It is a sign of disrespect. Don't get me wrong, I am not upset with you. To avoid your turning me down, I will wait here while you go and finish up your assignments. No matter how long it will take, I'll wait," he said.

It was a stare of shock that Boma shot at him. "No, sir. You shouldn't wait for me. I have a lot on my plate," she said. "I shouldn't keep you waiting, sir."

The man chuckled. "Don't worry, I am not complaining. But if you say you don't want me to wait, then don't make me wait. Just go in and get set and off we'll go."

She shook her head slightly. "I am not even in a good mood to go anywhere today. Please, sir, don't let me spoil your day," she said, trying to sound riled.

The big man drew his mouth downwards insouciantly, a sign that he was not moved by what she had just said. "If you spoil my day, it would not be new. I am ready to wait," he said with a stubborn smile. Then, he gave her a second look. "What is beating you up?"

She was glad he asked and she thought it was the best opportunity to push the guilt to him. "Actually, it is something you did and I have been too angry since I've heard it. I think it is better I just stay out of trouble and be on my own," she said, steeling up and trying not to mind that he was a social and political Hercules.

The smile disappeared from his face as he gave her a cool stare, his eyes unblinking, then his forehead furrowed and his eyes seemed to stab at her. She was intimidated by the stare as it seemed to question her temerity to talk to him in that manner. "And what could I have done, young lady?" he asked, his voice suddenly laden with a peremptory note.

She wilted for a moment but quickly regained her composure. "Sir, you offered my fiancé money to dump me. Is that not bad enough?"

Slightly, his eyes shifted out of a momentary guilt that he dispelled almost immediately. He returned his glare on her face. "And you believe that? I could test his love for you which truly I did. The question you should be asking is whether or not he failed the test."

She felt her head spin at the insinuation that Richard had possibly compromised. "He could not have failed. He told me what happened," she said.

The man laughed, loud and long, his laughter sounding like a wild bell in harmattan. "Let's go to his house and I will confront him."

"He has returned to Lagos."

The man laughed again. "So, he has run away after he failed," he said.

Boma was confused. Did it mean Richard lied to her? Did it mean Richard accepted the offer? She could not believe it. That broke her heart. She stared at the man, unable to muster the strength to pull the right chord to produce any word.

"Boma, I am still waiting for you," he said. Then he saw the tears in her eyes. "You don't need to weep over what isn't real. You should be happy that you found him out. I was never going to tell but since he did, I should speak out. He negotiated the money and when I told him he had failed a simple test that showed that he did not deserve you, he ran here to tell you a different story."

In the end, George's father was able hector her to go with him. She was very unhappy. She felt betrayed. Richard had betrayed her. Her heart was so heavy. George's father did not talk about Richard again; rather, he was telling her a story about when he first met her father in his youth. He was perceptibly trying to lighten her mood but she was lost in her dark thoughts of despair. She was just constantly fighting the tears back. *How could Richard?* she thought with a very heavy heart. She wished she was alone, locked up in her apartment, so she could cry out her pains.

George's mother was very happy to see her as she came to hug her. Boma was impressed by the grandeur of the house. It was a beautiful mansion with contemporary architectural design. There were many exotic cars in the compound and a large swimming pool by the side of the house. She tried to relegate the thought of Richard and his betrayal even as a new fear assailed her, the thought of being with George in his house and all that his parents were trying to do.

The woman led her inside and there were two pretty ladies and George in the living room. George smiled. Boma could tell that the ladies were his sisters. George rose with difficulty and came towards her. It seemed he wanted to embrace her but she extended her hand towards him for a formal handshake. He drooped and took her hand. It was a very brief contact and she walked forward to greet the ladies. They were happy to see her and they came forward to hug her. She hugged them.

George's father came in a few minutes later as he had been talking outside with the driver. He looked so cheerful.

"George, you can see that Boma is here. You must be grateful that she agreed to come and socialise with our family. Her family and ours are long-time friends. So, be repentant and treat her like the precious gem that she is," the man said.

Boma wondered what that meant. She would surely end this lunch with a sour taste for all of them.

The lunch was grand. There were many delicacies on the table. George was there sitting next to her but she said very few words to him. She had decided that there was just one way to spoil the fun and that was to keep talking about Richard and referring to him as her fiancé; that way, she would be able to keep so many issues at bay.

"I must say that I feel very excited to have Boma here. Look at her seated next to George like his queen. They look perfect together," his mother said, smiling.

Boma surprised them when she beamed a smile. They had not expected that because she had rarely smiled. "George was the most handsome man I knew until I met my fiancé," she said.

There was silence around the table. The family was staring at one another, confounded. Then George's father pushed back on his seat, obviously having lost his appetite. "George is still the most handsome young man. I've seen the man you call your fiancé, and I know him. He is a greedy young man who may have a comely face but his heart is prepossessing," he said.

Boma knew that the man was only trying to fight back. "Well, he is the sweetest young man I know; upright, very caring, and he makes such wonderful company."

Boma noticed that George's mother was very uncomfortable. She looked at George who was beside her. He was fidgeting with his food. The girls were the only ones eating heartily, even though, their eyes were darting about, probably disappointed at her.

"I hope you hear from your mother in Lagos," George's mother asked, trying to tactfully change the subject. Her husband was staring at Boma, his displeasure written all over his face.

"Yes, she sent messages to me through my fiancé as he came around and I have also responded to her message to assure her that I am fine and doing well," Boma said.

"What is this thing about this your fiancé? I thought you know how George feels about you," one of George's sisters who had been introduced to Boma as Cassy asked. Her name was actually Cassandra but she was simply called Cassy.

Boma smiled broader. “George? I know what George feels about every girl. He jumps from one girl to another,” she said.

George looked at her. “That is not true,” he protested. “You know you are the only girl I have truly loved and still love.”

“Really? You know I can mention a dozen of them in one breath,” she said and laughed, trying to sound innocent and jocose.

“Your mother knows that greedy young man who accepted the offer of money to leave you?” George’s father asked.

George’s mother grimaced. “Did he actually accept the offer?” she asked, looking lost. Boma saw that and she quickly cast her gaze on George’s father. He was trying to make a furtive sign to his wife when he noticed that Boma was staring at him. He forced a smile.

“Yes, he did,” he said.

That moment, Boma began to have second thoughts. However, she would worry about that later. For now, she just wanted George and his family to rue forcing her to their home to a lunch she did not need.

George’s mother did not push it and Boma assumed that she had finally got her husband’s cue.

"Such nasty behaviour," George said. "How could you be with a guy who is ready to accept money to dump you?"

"George, it is my fiancé you are talking about," Boma cautioned.

"He is not worthy to be your fiancé. You deserve a whole lot better than that. Such a character cannot guarantee your happiness," George said.

Boma was ready to hit him hard below the belt before his family members. "Neither can the one who was sleeping with my friend while he was dating me," she said.

There was a wave of shock that went around the table. From the shock, she noticed shame come upon George by his silence and then the embarrassment that came to his parents' faces.

"You did that?" George's father asked him.

George only bowed his head, quietened.

Nobody was ready to broach any topic because Boma was ready to torment them by bringing up her fiancé which she mentioned with glee. A few minutes later, when she had clearly quietened the family, she rose and thanked them for the lunch which she said she roundly enjoyed even though she ate only very little.

George's family just stared at her, defeated. His mother, however, nodded and said the driver would drop her but she declined, saying she wanted to stop by and see her fiancé's cousin on her way. It was a lie. She just wanted to dig into their wounds.

"The driver will still take you wherever you wish to go and he will ensure he takes you home safely," the woman said.

The woman's kindness softened Boma's heart. She felt sorry that she had behaved badly to her family but then, that was the only way she could have escaped the unwanted issues the lunch was planned to raise.

CHAPTER 22

Richard felt like a king knowing that he had won the heart of Boma. He went about with a smile on his face and it was easy for people around him to notice that he was very happy. Boma was a dream come true and he hoped that they would work out well. However, he missed her so much and he always thought of her. He wished there was a way he could reach her every day and talk to her. She had no telephone in school and he wished the much talked about era of mobile telephony for everyone had come to the country.

"You look so excited these days," Abiye said to him when he visited his friend at home. He went there because he wanted to see Boma's face from the large photo-frame on the wall. This was a week after he had returned from Port Harcourt. He and his friend had met like three times but this was the first time he was visiting. Abiye had expected that Richard would keep away from him because of Barbara's issue. Abiye was pestering him to forgive Barbara and take her back since she was desperately trying to reconcile with him.

“Well, I am just a happy soul,” Richard said and smiled rather too ebulliently.

Abiye smiled too. “I still want to talk to you about Barbara; that babe loves you and she is begging you to forgive her,” he said. Two days after Richard returned to Lagos, Abiye had gone to see him and had brought up Barbara’s issue. Barbara had been remonstrating over Richard’s breakup with her and was pleading for forgiveness because she loved him dearly. She had enlisted Abiye as his close friend to help her. Though Abiye knew it was near impossible for Richard to return to her because he was living out his character, he agreed to talk to his friend.

Richard had told him about the bad things Barbara was doing that he could not put up with. Abiye dismissed the allegation and vouched that Barbara could not be cheating on Richard. “Barbara is a very loyal person, perhaps, you overreacted,” Abiye had told him.

“Who did she tell you the Abuja politician is?” Richard had asked.

Abiye had shrugged. “She never mentioned anything about any politician,” he had said.

Richard had smirked. “What does that tell you? She is not being truthful. I cannot put up with her because she is seeing someone else. I talked to her about it. Why didn't she mention it to you? It is something that would surely come up when you come to talk to me about it and she knows it. She should have told you the complete truth," he had said.

Abiye had come back the following day and told him that Barbara denied it, that she just knew a politician who was nice and helpful to her by securing some works in the capital. Richard had laughed. He did not seem sad and that settled Abiye's conviction that Richard had used and dumped Barbara as it was in his character.

"The same politician she told me was her relative?" Richard had asked, amazed that the girl was telling lies. "Patrick, leave Barbara. She is not loyal, she is not faithful, she's not truthful and we have no future together." He was determined to push his point home so that Barbara would go away and clear the coast for his life with his newly won love.

Abiye had brought up the issue of Barbara again. Richard's eyes kept roving from his friend's face to the photograph on the wall where his Boma was smiling back at him. He wished he could have that photograph in his home. Then he wondered how Patrick would take it if he knew that his sister was the source of his joy and the strength he had derived to forget Barbara so easily.

Richard insisted that Barbara was a forgotten past to him and he would never have anything to do with her. "I won't allow someone who is not loyal and shouldn't be in my life to stand in my way and stop me from seeing the one who should be in my future," he said.

Abiye drooped but the topic changed because his mother walked into the living room. The boys talked about something else after greeting the woman. Richard kept staring at the photograph on the wall. That injected more joy in his heart. *This is what love is*, he said to himself.

In the next few days, Richard visited Abiye's house three times and Abiye wondered what the matter was. Richard was not caving in to his plea to accept Barbara back, yet he kept coming around. Abiye suspected something was amiss. Could it be that he was trying to get closer to Tonye? But then, Tonye was rarely at home when he came. So, what was he up to?

"You seem to be frequenting my house lately and you always barely spend more than ten minutes. What is going on?" Abiye asked him.

Richard smiled. "What is going on is that I now see a need to get closer to you because you are more or less my brother; a friend that is even closer than a brother," he said.

"You have always been close to me," Abiye said matter-of-factly.

"Yes, but you see, Patrick, I need you to see me as your friend, I see you as my best friend and I don't want what has happened between Barbara and me to affect our friendship in any way. I meant well but she blew it up," Richard said.

Abiye hung down his shoulders as he exhaled. "It won't, but it would be nice if you can forgive her. You should understand that a woman who makes mistake learns a lesson. She made a mistake by whatever she had done wrong to you. She understands how you feel about it and has learnt that vital lesson not to repeat it. Yours is to forgive," he said.

"Patrick, I have forgiven her but it is better to stay apart because trust is vital here and I can never trust her," Richard said. He stole a surreptitious glance at Boma's photograph on the wall. The sight of her lips and the recollection that he had kissed those sweet pink lips excited him and the joy surged up in him and diffused through his being. He smiled.

"Take that smile off your silly face," Abiye snapped at him. "You haven't made any sense in case you misconstrue that you just sounded like a sage."

Richard laughed because he knew he had fooled his friend. He wondered how enraged Patrick would be if he knew that he only came to his house to look at Boma's photograph and he was already in a relationship with his sister. He wished there was something he could do to make his friend not mind. He was afraid of doing anything at all.

A month had passed by since George's father had told Boma that Richard had negotiated with him to have money so he could walk out on her. However, after that disastrous lunch at George's house, Boma had reflected on all what had happened and had concluded that Richard could not have done that. She believed what Richard had told her instead. Though, many nights, she would still think about it and wonder if Richard had actually accepted George's father's offer. Certainly, it would shatter her heart if he did. She doubted he did, though.

She was preparing for her examinations that would commence in a fortnight. She was hoping to concentrate. She was anxious for the examinations to start and finish so she could travel to Lagos and be with Richard. She wished she knew where he lived in Lagos. She just would have gone to spend the holidays with him without her folks knowing that she was in town. She loved Richard so much, she told herself; and she would not allow anyone come between them, not George nor his seemingly nice but sly parents.

There would be a two day public holiday after the weekend. She toyed with the idea of going to Lagos for the weekend and public holiday but she discarded the thoughts. It would just be a waste because she wondered how Richard would know she was around and she might not see him before returning.

The following morning, she was preparing for school when a sharp knock came at her door. She wondered who it was. She went to the door and peeped through. Someone was standing there but she could not see his face because he was standing too close to the door, thus his face was above the peephole.

The knock came again and she asked who it was. "Boma, open up," the voice said. It was a familiar voice but she could not quickly identify it because the person spoke in low tones. She opened the door since she assumed it was someone she knew.

It was just as she opened the door that she remembered the voice but it was too late. She stared at him in shock, a grimace pleated her face.

"What are you doing here?" she asked.

"Please, let me come in. I cannot stand out here."

"This is not a place for you to come. Please, go away."

"Please, Boma. Don't do this to me. Whatever I did, I did it because of you. I was driven by an undying love for you."

Her face brimmed with indignation. "You better leave before I start shouting. Do you know the mess you put me in?" she yelled at him, irritated.

"Boma, please, I beg you," he pleaded.

She let out a sigh. She truly had nothing against him but what he did would make her unsafe if he stayed around her. "Dele, please, I beg you, just go away. I was arrested because of you. I don't want any trouble. Please, go!" She stepped back inside. She saw he made a move to push his way in but she quickly jammed the door and locked it.

"Open this door!" Dele yelled.

"My neighbours will call the police," she warned. That seemed to do the trick. She saw him through the window walking towards the road, a hood covering his head like a fugitive. He flagged down a motorcycle and went off. She was relieved. What was Dele up to? He was a wanted man, obviously. The police were out for him and so were George's friends. She wondered what he intended to do to her when he tried to burst his way into her apartment. She was scared.

CHAPTER 23

The news of the gunfight the night before was all over the school and environs and the first tale Boma heard that morning was that Dele Peters had been shot dead by the gunmen who attacked his hostel where he had returned to only a few days ago and was held up at. Boma had been too dazed and sad that she noticed that she was shaking at the news. Tears she could not control streamed down her face. That instant, she knew who had killed Dele. It was definitely George and his gang.

Dele had shown up at her place only four days earlier. Later that day, she had seen George and four boys in his car on campus. They drove past her. Fortunately, George did not stop to talk to her. She hoped he was still angry with her for the embarrassment she had hurled at him and his family during that lunch. She had imagined that a lot would have gone down afterwards and his parents and sisters would have told him to forget about her. They would have termed her as lacking in scruples and good manners. She hoped that was truly the case.

Then about an hour later, she had seen them in front of her faculty building. She was irritated because she wondered if George had nothing to do with his life to be roaming about school when it had been more than two years that he graduated. What attachment did he have with the school? His mates had done their national youth service and he was here loitering here.

George had not come out of the car. Two of the boys did and entered the building. She had gone her way. Then, that morning, four days later, as soon as she got to school, she had heard that there had been a gunfight and Dele had been killed. She was so sad and grief-stricken because Dele had been nothing but good and nice to her. She had not reciprocated his feelings but she did not hate him. He was her friend. Though she was disappointed that he was a cult boy and he had stabbed George, she did not hate him. If there was anything she would have wished him, it was his reformation. It was tough to imagine that Dele was dead.

She did not ask any question because she did not want to be linked to the fight that led to Dele's death. She was so disturbed and saddened by the news that she could barely concentrate that day. Then just as she was about to leave for her hostel, Sophia came into the class. She looked tired and worn out. She looked at Boma and walked up to her.

"Did you hear that there was a fight last night? Dele was shot twice," Sophia said.

A tear Boma could not hold back trickled down her right cheek, then in quick succession, more tears followed, cascading down both cheeks. She only nodded, sniffing as she fumbled with her handkerchief on her face.

"I have been at the hospital since morning. Dele is still in ICU battling for his life," Sophia said.

Boma stared at her in shock, everything in her being praying that what Sophia had said was true; that Dele was still alive. "He's alive?" she asked, hope rousing in her.

"Yes, he is alive and the bullets have been extracted from his body. He is, however, in critical condition. The doctors say his chances of pulling through are high," she said.

Boma prayed in her heart for Dele to survive. A ray of hope came upon her and she felt better.

"It is George and his notorious bunch. He refused to leave the school after graduation and he has come to constitute nuisance in this school," Sophia said.

Boma had nothing to say. She too had suspected that it had to be George and his gang but she did not have to say it so brazenly when she knew she had no proof. Besides, it was a cult fight.

"I guess you know why they attacked Dele?" Sophia asked. Boma frowned at the question but Sophia did not wait for an answer. "It was revenge for the fight where Dele stabbed George; the fight they had over you."

“Leave me out of this. They know why they had the fight. It has nothing to do with me and I don’t care about the two of them,” Boma said, suddenly indignant. She rose and walked out of the lecture hall. She did not know whether Sophia meant to make her feel guilty or make her feel better. She went home.

The following day, the news was all over the place that George had been arrested by the police after the school had filed a report. Unfortunately for George, his father was in Abuja and could not stop the arrest. By midday, it was on television and George had out of fear confessed to the crime. He even named those who accompanied him for the onslaught. The boys were arrested as well. By the end of that day, the school had responded by rusticating all the indicted students, Dele too was not spared.

Boma did not let George and Dele’s issue bother her. Once she knew that Dele had pulled through the next day after the gunfight, she moved on, mentally throwing them in a trash bin. She continued to prepare for her examinations. She had always been an outstanding student and she was determined to keep it up. She knew that George’s father would pull his son out of police net with his influence. It was the sad tragedy of the justice system in the country.

Boma was home that Saturday morning having light breakfast when a knock came at her door. She was not expecting anybody. She went to the door and peeped through the peephole. She could not believe her eyes and her heart began to race very fast. She flung the door open and screamed out in delight. She jumped into the arms of her visitor. She was over-excited.

"Richard! What are you doing in town?"

He smiled at her. "I missed you so much and once I realised that there would be a two-day public holiday after the weekend, I came to see you."

She was happy to hear that he had missed her. "I missed you too and I am very happy you are here," she said and hugged him again. She dragged him inside and then peeped out.

"Where's your car?"

"I didn't drive. I came by air," he answered.

She shut the door behind her as she faced him. Her Richard was here! She put her arms around his neck, he held her waist and she smiled brightly in his face. "You have just lifted my spirit by coming here," she said and she kissed him on his lips and so passionately that they almost choked. He held her tight as if he did not want to be separated from her, his own heart filled with the happiness that he had expected.

"I've been going to your house in Lagos and Patrick was beginning to be suspicious that he asked me why I was frequenting your house," Richard said. His face glowed with the joy he could not mask.

She was puzzled. “Why were you doing that?”

“I wanted to steal glances of your face from your photograph on the wall of your living room,” he said.

She giggled. “Isn’t that crazy?” she asked and they both laughed.

“That is how much I missed you. This time, we are going to take photographs together that I can always look at. I always wished I had a photograph of you in my bedroom, just by my bed. So, you would be the first thing I see in the morning and the last thing I see before going to sleep at night.”

She held him tight again.

After having a photo session on campus later that afternoon, they went to an eatery just in front of the main gate of the university and had lunch. Richard was always staring at her. Then, he asked her to tell him what had happened to her since he left.

She told him all that had happened. He was surprised that George’s father had told lies against him. However, he listened attentively till she finished. He wondered why the boys were fighting each other over her when he was the one guy she loved and wanted to be with.

Richard sighed. “First, I should respond to George’s father’s allegation against me. I am shocked that he would tell such shameless lies against a boy he is old enough to father. When he told me he would give me five million naira if I accepted to walk away from you, I told him that you were worth more than all the riches in this world and that was it. I never saw him after that day or had any contact with him," he said.

She stretched her arms across the table and held his hand with both hands; she squeezed gently. "It's okay, Baby. I believe you. The old man was only trying to paint you in bad light," she said. She reasoned that his explanation was consistent with what he had told her the first time.

He nodded. "I actually heard about George's issue. I met your friend at the airport when I arrived yesterday evening. She was on her way to Lagos. She recognised me and accosted me and told me a long story."

Boma was bemused. "My friend?" she asked.

"The one we saw the first time we went out to that restaurant when I picked you up from school."

Boma was puzzled because she could not recall what he was saying. She was wracking her brain when he mentioned the name. "She said her name is Tombra."

"Tombra is not my friend."

"Anyway, she met me at the airport and came over. She was cheerful and asked me when last I saw you. I told her I was just returning to town. Then she told me that George attacked Dele and shot him. That he got arrested and even his father was having problem trying to remove him from police net because George had admitted to the crime and the police commissioner is not friends with George's father," he said.

Boma did not know all this but she was not interested in it. She was disturbed that Tombra had stopped Richard to tell him all this. What was she up to? "Tombra is not my friend," she repeated to his surprise. "Why did she have to tell you all that?"

"I don't know. I wondered the same. She said she was going to work and live in Lagos. I was tired of her story that I had to excuse myself to leave."

Boma decided not to talk anymore about Tombra, even though she became worried that the girl was moving to live and work in Lagos, same city where Richard would return to in a few days. *I hope they never meet again,* she thought.

She had a great time with Richard in the few days that followed. She had insisted that he stayed with her in her apartment when he returned that Sunday and he did. They had moments of their own and it was the best moments of their lives. Memories were created and love was planted deeper.

CHAPTER 24

Towards the end of the year, Boma graduated. She had no issue as neither George nor Dele came to her. She did not see or hear from them though Sophia was always talking about going to see Dele but that had never interested her. She did not care about either of them. She was way past them.

She and Richard had nurtured their love in the past months and they had waxed stronger. She was completely in love and she had even suggested eloping should her family kick against their love. She had wanted to visit Lagos at the end of the first semester but Richard had told her not to bother because he thought they needed to still be discreet. She figured that she too was too excited that she might not have been able to manage it and her brother could easily find out. He had told her that her brother was still appealing to him to accept Barbara and Barbara was still begging. That disturbed her because she worried that Richard was under pressure to take Barbara back even though he had assured her that he would never do that.

Now, she was through with school and she was excited and anxious to return to Lagos. She left for Lagos that evening after she had defended and submitted her research project and was graded. She arrived in Lagos late and rather than go home, she took a taxi to the home address Richard had given her. She had two objectives in mind; first was to stay a day or two at his house before going home and the second was to catch him unawares since he did not know she was coming. She was able to locate the address.

Richard was home; she could tell from his car parked in front of the house. She went to the door and rang the bell. She could hear faint music coming from inside the house. The dulcet voice of Don Williams came, singing *"Listen to the Radio."* She smiled. Richard was just like her father, a lover of country music. She waited but no response came.

She pressed the bell again and there was still no response. She was sure this was the house because she recognised his car. What was happening? Was Richard with another girl and did not want to open the door? She became alarmed and her heart began to pound rapidly. She was hoping it was not true.

She pressed the bell the third time, this time long, still the door was not opened. Her heart fell as tears welled up in her. She felt a painful crack run through her heart. Sniffing to hold back the tears, she turned around and began to leave. She felt fooled. The car and music were her assurances that she was at the right place.

She was almost at the gate when she heard the door open. She turned and saw Richard standing at the door with only a towel wrapped around his waist, water dripping from his hair.

He was taken aback to see her. "Boma! It's you!" he said. He remained at the door, obviously not wanting to step beyond the door because he was almost naked and the neighbours should not see him like that.

Boma grimaced, as she stared at him. He beckoned at her and she walked back to him, her heart still pounding.

"I have been pressing the bell," she complained.

"I didn't know you were the one. I was in the bathroom and I was screaming, 'Give me a minute.' I thought it was Patrick because he's supposed to come and take me out this evening," he said. He pulled her with one arm and wrapped the arm around her shoulder. He took her inside.

"Which Patrick is coming to take you out?" she asked, still worried.

"Your brother! I actually thought he was the one pressing the bell," he said. He looked worried too. "Are you just returning from Port Harcourt?" He was looking at her bag.

"Yes. I finished today and took the evening flight," she said.

He smiled as he understood that she had come to his place instead. He embraced her and kissed her lips. “Congratulations, my love,” she said.

She wriggled out of his arms. “My brother is coming here. He mustn’t find me here,” she said. She was alarmed that Abiye would come there.

“Then, let me quickly get dressed and wait for him outside. When he gets here, we will go off. I will be back. I cannot cancel it because your brother is too smart,” Richard said.

Boma was sad at the realization that he would go out when she had come to stay with him. “What happens to me?” she asked.

He smiled. He carried her bag and led her to the bedroom. When he got there, he threw a vivacious smile at her again. “You are home, Boma. You will stay here and wait. Feel free. There’s food in the kitchen and check the refrigerator for whatever is there that you may want,” he said. He looked at the wall clock above the head frame of his bed. “Patrick will be here in no time.”

Boma sat on the bed and watched him as he got dressed. She was not angry. She was just thinking of the disaster it would be if her brother found her there. The outing they have would go up in flames.

“Where are you two even going?” she asked.

"He is inviting me out to a club," he said. "We go out most Fridays to hang out."

She nodded. "I hope you don't hang out with girls."

Richard laughed. "Not since I've met you."

"Before you met me?"

"Not really. I always had a girl with me. Your brother had a girlfriend he had dated for years but the relationship failed a few months ago because her mother doesn't trust Patrick," he said.

Boma was surprised. Of course, she knew her brother had a girlfriend but she did not know her as he never spoke of her or brought her home. He always had the disposition of the good guy. She remembered her father had once or twice asked him when he was bringing the girl he was dating home but Abiye had only laughed. Her mother too had talked to him about it and her brother had told their mother that he was only interested in going abroad for his masters. She wondered why he still had not gone because the plan had been on for long.

"They broke up because of her mother?" Boma asked, puzzled.

"Your brother went to the embassy and was denied the visa because her mother, who was aware that he was trying to leave to study abroad, had written to the embassy. Like I said, she did not trust him. She thought he was too handsome to be serious and his travelling out was a way to run away from her daughter after fooling her all these years," he said.

Just then, the doorbell rang. They exchanged glances. "You stay here. I will be gone for two to three hours. There's a spare key in the bedside drawer, he said. He had his jeans trousers on. He slipped on his collared yellow tee-shirt and picked up his shoes. He dashed into the living room just as the bell rang again.

In the living room, he slipped into his shoes and opened the door. Patrick was there.

"What's keeping you? You are not ready?" he asked as he walked into the room rather hastily.

"What is the matter? Is someone chasing you?" Richard asked.

"I am pressed and I need to take a leak," Patrick said. He entered the visitor's toilet next to the living room. Richard heaved a sigh. He quickly dashed into the bedroom and wore his cologne. He gestured to Boma to remain calm and he went back out to the living room. His friend was just coming out of the toilet.

Patrick looked at him somewhat quizzically. "Are you with someone?" he asked.

Richard was not sure how to respond and wondered what he had done to give away that he was not alone. "I am alone. Why do you ask?"

"When I came in, I smelt a feminine scent, something like jasmine. You know I have sisters and I know such fragrances," Patrick said.

Richard kept a straight face in his earnest effort to shroud his unease. "Oh, I see. Maybe it was the lady that came here earlier to deliver the soup I ordered," he said, the lie coming with ease and it amazed even him. "Let's go."

Just at the door, Patrick stopped and looked down. Richard saw what had caught his friend's attention; a pair of female slip-ons. His heart began a rapid palpitation as he feared that Patrick would recognise the shoes. Patrick looked at him with a crinkly face.

"I thought you said you are alone?" Patrick asked. He was staring straight at him, askance. "What are you hiding from me?"

Richard tried to be as calm as possible. He looked at the shoes and chuckled. "A girl was here last weekend and she left her shoes behind. I think she will be back in a few days from now."

Patrick guffawed. "Another victim?" he asked.

"Come on, shut your mouth up," Richard said and playfully pushed Patrick out of the house. His heart was beating and even he felt tremulous as they walked to Patrick's car; it was actually one of his father's.

Boma was relieved when she heard the car's engine rev to life and she knew when it drove off. She went to the front window and peeped through. The car had driven away. She looked down at her shoes. She sighed. She was happy that her brother had not recognised the shoes. He was actually the one who had gifted her the shoes on her birthday two years ago. Of course, it was outlandish to think that she would be the one that was there. He would not suspect that. However, she had her fears. Abiye was a smart young man, he was also very reflective. He could think it over later and in retrospect link the jasmine fragrance to the shoes. She hoped he never did.

She went to the kitchen. She was impressed how organised Richard was. His house was very neat and she was almost smiling when a thought hit her. *What if there was a lady who did all this for him?* She heard all the quick responses he had given Abiye. If they were lies, it meant Richard was a very smooth liar. Could she trust such a character? Was she not getting herself into a dangerous situation that could leave her shattered in the end? She shook off the thoughts. She would trust him and believe that he would not break her heart. He was the one man she had been in a relationship with for the longest time, seven months, a month more than George. The only difference was that she had not spent as much time with him as she had spent with George and she could not say she knew him very well.

She found freshly made okra soup with seafood. She was happy. She fixed a meal for herself and afterwards, she sat to watch television only for her to doze off in less than ten minutes. She was very tired after a long day.

CHAPTER 25

Boma spent two days at Richard's house. It was a memorable two days and she loved every moment of it. Richard spent the whole of Saturday indoors with her and she wished the moments would last forever. On Sunday evening, she had gone home in a taxi.

Her parents and siblings were surprised because they had not expected her as she had not informed them that she would be coming. Her father was particularly baffled because she had always informed him ahead, so he could send a driver to collect her from the airport. However, they welcomed her.

Later that night while she was in her room, her mother came and sat beside her on the bed. "I learnt you met one of my secondary school best friends in Port Harcourt," the woman said.

Boma's head spun. She had intended not to mention George's mother to her or anyone in the family. She stared at her mother for a moment. "Your secondary school best friend?" she asked, feigning loss of memory.

"Yes. She said she met you and even took you to her house. George's mother. You know George at least," her mother said.

"Oh!" Boma exclaimed. "George's mother! She did not take me to her house. It was her husband who came to pressure me to go to their house for lunch against my wish," she said, her nose and mouth contorted into a sneer of disdain.

Her mother noticed the displeasure in her. "You don't seem to like her. She is a nice person. She always looked out for me in secondary school," her mother said. Then she smiled teasingly. "So, I heard you and her son were an item in Port Harcourt."

Boma made a face of disgust. "No, we were not. We were just friends for a while but he is a bad boy. He is into campus cult and he is a terrible womaniser, chasing everything in skirt. I didn't like him. He was arrested some months back after he almost killed somebody. He graduated over two years ago yet he kept coming to school to foment trouble," she said. Her intention was to quickly make her mother dislike George's character in case his mother had painted him as a wonderful kid that was usually misunderstood.

“Really?” her mother asked. “But I learnt you dated him and broke up with him because you saw him talking with another girl.”

Boma’s eyes rose and looked at her mother, then, she wilted upon the realization that her mother must have known more than she thought. She decided to tell her mother the story. Of course, she omitted Richard’s part. It was just George and his silly lifestyle.

Her mother did not seem outraged by her story. When she was done, the older woman just beamed at her. “Life is not the way we see it. Again, people change as they grow older. George could just have been sowing his wild oats as a young boy then, that doesn’t mean he has not changed,” she said.

Boma was shocked at her mother’s words. She had expected the woman to write the boy off and tell her such a character was one she must avoid at all cost.

“I see your coming together with George as reuniting our families. We have been long-time friends. George’s parents came to find us and they have shown interest in you,” her mother said.

Frustration crept up in Boma’s heart. How could her mother say such? She had thought she was over with George. Why did he always pop up? He was a past she had been running away from and he had somehow been coming up again and again that he had become more of a nightmare. Now, he had reached her family.

"I know George. I can never have anything to do with him," she said.

"Why? You can't continue to hold grudge against him for a mistake he made in his growing up days," her mother said.

"George was grown when I met him. He was gallivanting and living large. He was living his life; not making mistakes. He was jumping from one girl to another and sleeping with my friends. He respects nobody," she said.

Her mother shook her head. "That's bad of him but I believe he is repentant now and wants you back. His family and ours are here to whip him into line if he misbehaves, which I know he would not," she said. "By the way, who is the young man I'm told you're seeing who accepted to collect money to walk away from you?" her mother asked.

Boma deliberately gave her mother a shocked look. "That is not true. Nobody accepted to take any money to walk away. George's father just made that up," she said.

"Who is the young man?" her mother asked.

Boma noticed that she had begun to sweat in her palms. Telling her mother the truth would be exposing their secret. Just then, Abiye walked in. He was smiling.

"I wish you returned earlier. You would have met my fiancée. Her name is Jessica," he said.

Boma was amused. "You have a fiancée and you finally brought her home? Wow! I always wondered if you ever had a girlfriend," she said. It was her escape from answering her mother's question.

He laughed. "She is a nice girl, very clean," he said.

"But she is not beautiful. I expected a more beautiful girl for you," their mother said.

"Mum, beauty is in the heart," he said.

The woman shrugged. "That girl looks timid but I'm sure she is pretending being that it was her first time here. She was too quiet but you could see in her eyes that she was smarter than she tried to act," she said.

"Mummy, she is a cool lady," Abiye said.

His mother shrugged. "Well, time will tell," she said. She got up and left the room.

Boma was relieved. Her mother had either forgotten her question or had postponed it for another time but it provided the relief for her at the moment. She turned to her brother, starry-eyed. "Wow! Tell me about her. Is she nice? Is she beautiful? Is she someone who can get along with you?"

Abiye laughed. "She is sweet and I love her is all I can say, but wait until you see her," he said. "She will come around soon. She is actually Barbara's cousin. You remember Barbara? Richard's girlfriend?"

Boma stared at her brother in shock. Her brother saw the look. She realised herself and looked away. "Isn't Barbara the lady we met at the supermarket a certain time around Christmas last year?" she asked.

He nodded. "Yes, she is," he said.

She forced a smile but which came rather mechanically. "That exquisitely beautiful lady I always think of and admire. She's divinely beautiful," she said. Then she paused as if she recalled something. "But I thought you said Richard dumped her."

"Yes, he did. He explained some things to me but the girl is not giving up on him. I've told her that Richard is done with her but she has refused to accept. She said she loves him so much. I think Richard has moved on and doesn't think about her. I have tried my best to tell her to forget him but she said she will not forget him, and believes that with time, he will go back to her, so long as she never gives up," he said.

A sigh of relief escaped from her throat. "Poor lady! She should just move on with her life if he is no longer interested in her."

Her brother was staring at her now. "I hear you had a very handsome boyfriend in school and he is Mummy's secondary school best friend's son."

She went agape. Did everyone in her family know about it? "He just fooled me because I was in my first year and did not know any better. He is a terrible guy. He was sleeping with my friends and was disrespecting me by keeping other girls. He made me a fool. The relationship lasted for only six months. I had to break up with him because of all his transgressions," she said.

"I hear he has repented," Abiye said.

"A cult guy who almost killed a boy I know? He is very vicious and violent." She needed to make George look very horrible and unacceptable.

"He's a bad guy then. Such a guy won't make a good partner," he said. "It's good you dumped him. My fear is that you will have some pressure to reconnect with him. Don't let anyone force you to accept what you don't want. Just go for what you want."

Boma was happy to hear that. She thanked and hugged her brother.

"So, tell me, who is the new guy? I hear he comes from Lagos," he asked. He was smiling.

Her heart missed a beat and began to thump. She rubbed her palms on her dress. "You heard all that too?"

"George's mother came to find Mummy after you met. She was very happy and they talked and she told her everything. Actually, she wants you reconciled with her son because she really loves you."

"Anyway, he's just a friend. I'm sure, with time, you will meet him."

***

Boma did not see Richard all through the week. Richard had told her that he would not come to her house and she must be careful not to come to his house except she wanted them to be found out. They had agreed to meet at a private place away from their homes. Now, Boma was thinking it was better to spill out the truth to her family because it was better to start the fight early than to delay now that George's mother had found her mother and had come with tales. Though her mother did not ask her about the unknown man in her life again, it seemed she was angling for George.

Then she had noticed that her mother was always whispering something to her sister and she had wondered what they were talking about and why they were whispering. Whenever she walked into a room where her mother and sister were, they would go quiet. Then, she did not understand why Tonye was always canvassing for George. Tonye had never met George but she talked as if she had always known him.

"George is a great guy, a chap born with a silver spoon. He has everything a woman needs in a man. Then, he is humble enough to seek for forgiveness where he erred. Such a man is rare in this part," Tonye had told her two days after her arrival.

Boma had deliberately refrained from talking about George because she had told her family how horrible a character he was. Except for Abiye, they all seemed not to mind his bad behaviour. Her father was always talking about his friendship with George's father and how he and his wife had helped him back then to convince her mother to marry him.

Boma was tired of hearing such stories. Nothing about George interested her. He was no good to her. She decided not to mind them. Now, Saturday morning, she had decided to visit Richard at home knowing that he would be home. Her brother had been home the night before, which meant they did not hang out that Friday night as they often did. She told Tonye that she wanted to visit her friend from school.

Tonye became worried. "Can't you go another day? You should stay home today," she said.

"I just want to go out today," Boma said.

"Then, you have to be home in time; at least, before two pm," Tonye said.

"What is happening, Tonye? You and Mummy have been up to something and I am honestly suspicious."

Tonye looked surprised at her then, consciously, she let the astonishment disappear from her face after realising it. She looked around as if she wanted to make sure no one was close by. She drew closer to her younger sister. "Mummy doesn't want anybody to know until two pm but I can tell you for free if you promise not to betray me."

"What is it? You can always trust me."

Tonye lowered her voice. "My fiancé, a soldier, is coming to propose this afternoon and Mummy wants it to be a surprise to you and Abiye. I don't know why but that is what she wants."

Boma smiled. She was genuinely happy for her sister. She did not know who the man was but she was not in any mood to talk longer than necessary. She just wanted to see Richard and she was so anxious about it that she wished to have been gone already. "Don't tell me anything about him. I will wait till I meet him then you will spend this evening telling me more about him," she said gleefully.

CHAPTER 26

Richard wished for just one thing as he laid on the hard tiled floor of his living room: to see Boma. He missed her so much. It was painful that he could not see her even though she was in Lagos. If only she had remained in his house and had not returned home, he would have been having the time of his life with the girl he loved so completely and so truly.

He sat up with a decision to take a risk to visit Patrick at home. He would at least see Boma even if they did not talk, but he would be happy. Just as he was making up his mind, the doorbell rang. He was startled. He went to the door and opened. He grimaced at whom he saw. She was the last person he expected at his place.

She beamed at him; her smile was so charming and captivating. “Hi Richie,” she said and glided past him into the house before he could snap out of his initial bewilderment.

"What do you want here?" he asked her. He remained at the door, staring back at her.

She tittered. "I came home to my beau," she said.

"Barbara, I am not your beau and I have told you to stay out of my life. I'm not interested," he said, the pitch of his voice rose almost to the point of explosion. He was obviously livid with anger from the way he stared at her.

Barbara walked back to him and smiled into his face, defiantly. "Richie, Baby, you know I have no other life besides you. I have been begging you to forgive me since end of last year. I don't even know what exactly I did wrong to you. I have said, whatever it is that I have done, I am sorry and I am willing to make amends," she said, allowing her body to melt into his.

Richard looked into her beautiful face. "I have forgiven you. It's just that I have moved on with my life. I don't go back. I am a forward moving person," he said.

She put her arms around his neck. "Stop being difficult, Richard. I fight for what I want and I don't ever give up," she said. "You will marry me."

Richard stepped back, removing her arms from around his neck. He gave her a cool stare, his nose turning up at her. "I will marry you? Do you have charm in your mouth? Well, I refused to be bewitched. Please, the door is still open," he said and snapped his head towards the door.

She rushed at him and held on to him. “Richard, please, don’t do this to me, I beg you. My life has never been the same,” she said, suddenly sobbing.

“I am not moved by pity, I’m sorry. You can be my friend but forget anything happening between us.”

She stared at him amidst her teary eyes. Then, she moved backwards and stoned him with a tough look. “There will be nobody for you, Richard. Nobody! It is either me or nobody else for you,” she said in sheer anger.

“Please, leave,” Richard bawled. She was frightened.

***

Richard was agitated when the doorbell rang again. He sighed and hesitated. The bell rang yet again. He had been prancing about the living room a few minutes earlier. He went to the door, ready to yell at whom he thought was there. He froze when he saw Boma.

“Boma!” he said, trying to calm himself down. He took a deep breath and exhaled noisily.

Boma looked at him strangely. He looked worked out. “What is the matter with you? Have you been fighting?” she asked. She looked behind him to see if he was with somebody. She entered the house and looked around. Her sharp nostrils caught the soft, sweet vanilla fragrance. Instantly, she knew that a woman was in the house.

"You have a guest?" she asked, staring at him in utter apprehension.

He shook his head. "No, I am alone," he answered. He still looked ruffled.

She grimaced as she stared at him, trying to decipher answers from his eyes. She got none. She walked into the bedroom and looked around; nobody was there. She went to the other room; nobody was there. He was right behind her.

"What are you looking for?" he asked. "You don't trust me when I say I have no guest?"

"I know a woman is here. Where is she hiding?" she said, still looking around in case the woman was hiding.

"No woman is here but if you care to know, one was here."

She was frozen. She turned like a creaky door to face him. "Which woman was here?" she asked. Her heart was already quickly breaking. Was this what it meant to be in love with a heartbreaker? Why had she allowed herself into this emotional morass?

"Calm down, Boma," he said.

"Who is she?" she insisted.

Richard sighed. She was staring at him and that sigh roused irritation in her. "It's Barbara. She came here to plead with me but I sent her away," he said.

"Barbara was here?" she asked. He nodded. "What did she come here for? So you are still seeing her? Why are you then deceiving me?" she yelled at him, peevish.

He grabbed her upper arms. "Stop it, Boma! Listen to me! Yes, she came here a while ago. I sent her out. I didn't even know you would be here. I don't have anything to do with her," he said.

Her eyes settled on his. She could see only toughness in his eyes even though they were pleading with her for understanding. He saw fear and insecurity in her eyes and he wondered why she would ever have any fears with him. Then tears trickled down her face. He pulled her close into his arms, their bodies liquefying into each other. "Please, Boma, believe me, I will never do anything to hurt you. I love you so much," he said.

She remained still, her hands held up against his chest, restraining them from wrapping around him. Her doubts did not abate. Then, she thought of her discussion with her brother, how Barbara was still after Richard and did not want to give up. She felt guilty and ashamed that she had reacted hastily. Her guilt nudged her and in an instant, she melted, her arms dropped and then moved around his back. She held him, her face buried in his chest.

"What does she want?" Boma asked.

"She came to plead for me to accept her back but I told her it is impossible."

She raised her head to see his face. "Richard, will you ever leave me?" That instant, she remembered she had been in a similar situation with George back then and she had asked the same question. George had assured her he would never leave her, yet, he left the day she caught him and Tombra in that uncompromising position at the bar.

"Boma, just trust me that I will always be with you. I will never leave you."

Her eyes were still cast on his face. "Leaving me could come as doing something that would make me leave you."

He frowned. "You want to leave me?"

She shook her head. "No, I would never do that but I will if I ever met you with another girl. Love is beautiful but once it is disrespected, it means it is not appreciated and once I feel that way, love deserts my heart." She wondered if this could ever happen with Richard. She had heard stories about him that ought to have made her not bother about him but she could not stop yearning for him.

He was about to say something but she put a finger on his lips. "It's okay, we are fine," she said, suddenly brightening up, "I'm sorry I reacted that way. I am just so much in love and don't want to be hurt," she said.

Her sudden glow was infectious. He beamed too. They hugged tightly for a moment and allowed their lips and tongues to greet each other rather passionately. She felt her legs wobble as the passion surged up in her. His hands were moving around her body and she knew things would happen. She suddenly pulled her head back and pushed him away.

"Calm down Mr. Wolf," she said jocosely.

He laughed but said nothing. His eyes were alit and they were already eating her up, his hard breath showed. She walked away from him and sat on a sofa. He came over and sat beside her.

"It's been one long week. I was almost dying because I missed you so much," she said.

"It was worse for me. I was not only lonely; I felt a sense of depression. I longed to see you and I was struggling with the thoughts of going to your house to see you. Even if I would not talk to you."

"We can't continue like this. We love each other. We should not be hiding what we have," she said ruefully.

"I am trying to protect my friendship with your brother. He would fight me. He would hate me," he said.

"Whatever he would do, there's no time he would not do it. Why postpone the evil day?" she said.

He struggled with his confusion. It would be disastrous if Patrick found out. He was sure that Patrick would never accept him. For him, it was a desecration of their friendship to have any feelings for his sister much more having a romantic relationship with her. It would be impossible to convince him on that. “This will be very difficult. I know your brother. I think he is still trying to secure another visa to one of these European countries. Once he gets it and he leaves, then we are free,” he said.

“My brother is not going anywhere anymore. He has joined my father’s business,” she said.

Richard was quiet. She was an insider and should know better. He got up and began to pace about the room. She watched him as she waited. He should come up with a solution.

“What if we do it this way? Work your travelling to the United States. I will do likewise. We will go there, get married and everything will be history,” he said.

She was not impressed by his idea. “What about my youth service year? I am waiting for that.”

He stared at her for a long moment. Then he smiled. “Good. Once you go on youth service, I will try and work my transfer to wherever you are posted to. Before anybody realises it, we would be married.”

She sighed. “It is not as easy as that. I just think we should not deny ourselves of seeing each other because of my brother,” she said. “I thought you said you were ready to take the risk and whatever consequence that came with it.”

He expelled the air in his lungs. “Boma, please, it is better not to stir the beehives. We should be able to take it one step at a time. Give me time to think about a strategy,” he said.

She decided to change the topic. She told him about her sister’s fiancé who was coming to their house for lunch and how her parents were making preparations. He was pleasantly surprised. He surprised her when he told her he had met Tonye’s man.

“He is a good looking young man. He is a military officer and gentleman to the core,” he said.

Boma was surprised because she did not know anything about her sister’s fiancé and she had never met him or even knew what he looked like. Anyway, she would see him later that day.

CHAPTER 27

Boma did not stay long at Richard's place. Once it was a quarter after two pm, she left. She told him she would come back the following day. He agreed that he would take her out, far to where nobody knew them. It was beginning to look like an exciting adventure; loving in secret and running away to avoid being noticed. She smiled at the thought.

There were two big cars parked in her compound and it just meant that they had visitors. She was happy for Tonye because she assumed that, from the cars, her fiancé was wealthy. Two cars meant that there was more than just one person, obviously a family. She had wondered earlier about her sister's fiancé coming to propose. What kind of proposal was that? She had not had time to reflect about it because her mind had been centred on visiting Richard. This was a marriage introduction, it seemed.

Her mother met her as she entered the house. The reproachful look in the woman's eyes told her that her mother was displeased. She greeted her mother.

"Where did you go?" her mother asked her with her nose hung up in irritation.

"Didn't Tonye tell you that I went to see a friend?" Boma said.

"You should have asked me for permission, not Tonye. I needed you to be around."

Boma feigned confusion. "I didn't know that. What is going on?" She did not want her mother to know she had an idea.

"What is going on is that you were supposed to be home and you needed to have taken permission from me before going out," her mother said sternly.

Boma was annoyed. "Mummy, I am not a child. I am a graduate."

"You are my child and you live under my roof," her mother said. Then as if she had been consoled by some invisible divine hands, she relented and smiled at her daughter. "Anyway, welcome back." She embraced her.

That sudden switch confounded Boma. Her mother held her hand and led her into the living room where the guests were. She wanted to protest that she could not go and meet Tonye's fiancé and family like that—that she needed to freshen up—but the better part of her whispered that she needed not raise unnecessary issues with her mother.

"Here comes my beautiful daughter, Boma Horsfall," her mother announced as soon as they entered the living room.

Boma froze as she saw the people in the living room. The Douglases! She stared at them as if they were people she had seen in a nightmare the night before. They were smiling at her. George seemed to have changed his looks. He looked athletic, fit, and very charming in his new haircut. However, that did not impress her in anyway. His parents were smiling at her. His father rose to welcome her. Boma refused to move beyond the door. She pulled her hand from her mother's hold.

"Surprise!" Tonye said, throwing her hands toward George and his parents.

Boma cast a hateful look at her sister. She felt betrayed. If she had thought anyone could betray her, she never thought Tonye could.

"We invited George and his parents over for lunch as a surprise for you," her mother said, smiling. Boma turned to her mother. She could see the woman's eyes were pleading with her not to disgrace her and the family. She succumbed to those pleading eyes.

Boma forced a smile that did not improve anything in her but overtly accentuated the pretence it was meant for.

"Wow! This is a surprise. I did not expect this," she said. Her eyes met George's and she fired her disapproval at him. She held up the gingerly smile that mocked even the intention.

George's father came forward and hugged her in with his massive frame; the strong musk fragrance he wore almost choked her. She liked men who smelt like this but this was not the moment to like anybody.

"Good to see you, Boma, my daughter," he said.

She cringed within. Then she saw her father smiling at her. She was in trouble! These people were all up to set her up to accept George. As soon as George's father released her, she stepped forward toward his wife and greeted her. She still carried the fake smile that had become embarrassing even to a keen observer.

Even George wished she could do without the smile because it put them all on edge. He rose as soon as she had greeted his mother who had embraced her. He was posed to embrace her as well. She gave him a brief glance and threw a brief greeting and turned away. She walked towards the door.

"Where are you going? We are about to have lunch. We were waiting for you," her mother who was still standing close to the door said.

"I just need to freshen up," Boma said and exited the living room. She practically ran all the way to her room upstairs. She was angry. She did not like what was happening. Why could George and his parents not accept that she was not disposed to them? She and George could never get together. Never again!

She was restless as she pranced about the room, many thoughts rousing and colliding against one another in her head. She did not want to have lunch with the Douglases, yet she knew that would embarrass her parents. She wondered where Abiye was. Was he not part of this too? Tonye! So, Tonye had fooled her so she could return home in good time. She would not have bothered if she knew George and his parents were coming. Her leaving the house that morning would have been her perfect escape! Tonye had betrayed her by that sheer deception.

Just then, a gentle knock came at the door. She answered. It was her father. He came in. He looked at her with strange eyes.

"What are you doing?" he asked. The man could see how tensed and disturbed she was.

She threw her face away. "Nothing, sir," she muttered almost to herself.

"I thought you said you were coming up to freshen up," the man said. He had aged rather quickly. Boma had noticed when she returned home last week. He had lines of exhaustion around his eyes and she wondered what the matter was. Her father, a workaholic, had always been full of life and youthfulness, always having some business he was doing since he left the medical practice some years ago. He had boundless energy that seemed never-ending and that was one thing she most admired about her father; he was hardworking and his mind was always busy not on profitless exercises.

“Yes sir,” she said tersely.

“What is the matter? You don’t look happy,” he observed.

“There’s nothing to be happy about,” she said, her face still averted.

“And I am sure there’s nothing to be unhappy about as well,” he said.

She took this opportunity. She returned her face and her eyes fixed on him. The unfamiliar lines were still there and she feared that he was getting too old. He was sixty-five, she realised.

“There’s everything to be unhappy about,” she said, her eyes pleading for understanding.

“What is the matter, Honey?” he asked.

“Why are these people here? What is going on? Tonye told me her fiancé was coming over to meet with the family. Why are The Douglases here?” she asked.

Her father's shoulders sank as he forcefully expelled air from his lungs. "They are our friends from way back and we are happy to be reuniting after so many years. I could have reached Chief Douglas long ago when he was minister but I was too occupied with my medical practice and you know I am one person who does not accept that people should use political offices to favour family members and cronies," her father said.

"But their son is a thug," she said.

Her father raised a brow. "Is he?"

"Yes, a notorious one," she said. She would not say anything good about George since he did not want to disappear from her life.

Her father sat on her bed. "Why do you say that of him? He looks like a respectable young man. My friend would not have raised such a character."

She shrugged. "He was in a cult; he beats people; and he shot someone who almost died. He was even arrested."

Her father's shoulders dropped again. "I think his father told me. It was a mistaken identity. George was not even there when it happened. People just thought he had a hand in it and that was why he was arrested. He was released and the police apologized to him," he said. He looked very exhausted even now and his voice shook.

“His father told you that?” she asked. She had ensconced it in her mind that George’s father was a pathological liar and that was disappointing to her. He was a typical politician.

“Boma, we will talk about this later. For now, quickly freshen up and join us. Do not embarrass us with any untoward behaviour. We are a respectable family,” he said, giving her a stern look that reminded her that his words were law and she was not expected to violate them so long as she was his child.

Painfully, she nodded.

Without another word, he rose and walked out of the room. Boma was frustrated. Then, she had an idea. There was always a way to treat such matters.

CHAPTER 28

Boma almost fainted when George's father brought up Richard in his discussion. She had been very quiet all through the lunch. George sat next to her. She wore a caustic smile. Every now and then, her father would throw a look at her but she would intentionally not look at him. Her mother and her girlhood friend were chatting when, suddenly, the former ambassador asked her about Richard. Fortunately, he did not remember his name. He just said, "How is that boyfriend who agreed to collect money to walk away from you?"

Boma was silent for a moment. Her mind was running riot and she wished she could yell out her indignation. "He did not agree to collect money. He had told me what transpired even before you mentioned it to me. You made the offer and he told you that I was worth more than all the wealth in the world," she said.

George's father was shocked. He shook his head as if he wanted to wipe off dizziness from his eyes. He looked silly for a moment as he looked around the table. Then, he made a quick frantic effort to comport himself, chuckling to bid time. "Wow! That means he lied to you. He said five million naira was a lot of money and he would accept the money. What do you expect? That he would tell you that he accepted to collect money in exchange for you?"

Boma smiled; this time the smile beamed real. "Anyway, you asked how he is. He is very fine, thank you, sir," she said.

"How come you have a boyfriend that is unknown to this family?" her father queried.

"Daddy, I just got back," she said. "He will come around at the right time."

Her father's face steeled. He was staring intently at her and she wondered if she had done anything thus far to disgrace the family. "Once a good girl has a boyfriend, her family should know," he said. "He should have at least come to see us so we know who is visiting our daughter in school."

Boma was silent. She did not want to argue with her father. Her father was a very good, kind man; very doting and she loved him so much. It would amount to disrespect if she argued with him in front of his phony friends from the past. The fact that George's father lied made him a fake friend.

"I want to see that young man before midday tomorrow," her father said.

Boma was shocked. Trouble alert! She began to cringe; her hands were beginning to shake. “Erm... erm... Sorry, Daddy, he cannot make it tomorrow. He is not in town. He travelled to Accra on official assignment,” she said.

“And he is probably enjoying himself with those bulky Ghanaian ladies. They are an exotic beauty, pretty faced with massive backsides that get young men easily tempted,” George’s father said shamelessly.

“Oh, stop it!” George’s mother chided him and looked at Boma. “We are not here to discuss the young man. You know I personally love you from the first minute I saw you. Then I was happy that you are the centre of my son’s life. He was always talking about you. Then, when I met you, I just knew that you were the right lady for my son. Then fate even has it that you are my best friend’s daughter. It’s a reunion of families. We are good friends and now, we will become family. We just want you to forgive George and let bygones be bygones. Look into the future; there will always be better days,” she said.

Boma was heaving as she listened to the beautiful woman. She would have loved George’s mother and be friends with her had she not been George’s mother or had she accepted her decision that she and her son were history.

“Boma, you should start considering George, he is a fine young man and I like him,” her mother said.

Boma turned to George. He had been very quiet. He gave her an uneasy smile. "George, do you mind to tell them that you were a thug back in school? Tell them the truth what you did with my friends and why I left you," she said.

George bit the corner of his lower lip nervously. "I made silly mistakes because I didn't know any better. I realise my silly mistakes and I have learnt from them," he said.

"That's it! A real man realises his mistakes, admits them and learns from them," her father said.

Boma made efforts to contain her frustrations. "George, just tell them what you did and were still doing even while you were begging for forgiveness? It is a man who is truly repentant that deserves forgiveness, not the one who says he is sorry yet continues to do the same wrong deed," she said.

"Whatever I did then was borne out of my youthful exuberance. I am sorry I made such silly mistakes and I promise I will never make such mistakes again because I am older and wiser," George said.

"So, you call the choice of being a thug a mistake?"

"Boma, he has said he is sorry for his mistakes," her father reproached her.

She decided to go back to her initial plan. To be mute, especially now that the discussion had veered to the main reason for the unsavoury lunch.

Tonye was staring at her sister and saw that she really disliked George. He must have really hurt her. She also knew that Boma was angry with her for deceiving her that it was her fiancé who was coming around. She noticed that Boma was now avoiding making eye contact with her. She felt terrible and was unhappy.

"Boma, forgiveness heals all wounds and restores love and makes it even stronger," her mother said; her voice gentle and patronising.

Boma only nodded. In her head, she wondered what was there to forgive. She had no grudge against George; she was only just done with him. She now had Richard who was rocking her world. Was Richard the problem why she could not accept George? Certainly not! For more than two years before she met Richard, she had refused all George's entreaties.

Her parents and George's parents were throwing counselling words at her and George, talking about love, forgiveness, family, and the need to maintain family friendships. She just sat mute, listening but revolting in her head. Nothing they said made sense to her. She could never imagine herself being with George. She might have hated him for some time after she found him out with Tombra but that hate had long dissipated and she just felt nothing towards him. His efforts at constantly trying only formed into irritation to her.

In the end, the parents and Tonye excused themselves, so Boma and George could have the time and space to talk. *Such a futile enterprise,* Boma thought. She was not going to break her silence.

“So, Boma, you heard everything our good parents have said. We make mistakes but what is important is that we learn vital lessons of life from the mistakes. I am eternally sorry for my stupidity back in school. I assure you that I will never do anything to hurt you again,” he said. He was watching her. She sat there unmoved and speechless.

“I know I drove you to find another man but I have always been there with you, always loved you and still loving you. You are everything that matters to me,” he said. He drew closer to her.

She winced in her head, dreading any physical contact with him.

“Come on, Baby, let’s not fail our parents. We should make them happy. Our being together would make them happy,” he said.

She wanted to sneer but restrained herself.

She saw him move and then he touched her, his fingers pressing against the skin around her neck. She jolted and slapped his hand away. She eyed him with stern disapproval. He was deflated by that. He turned away. He looked helpless. When he turned to her again, he went on his knees and began to plead with her.

“Please, Boma, I am on my knees. Forgive me. Take me back as your love so that I may live again. You are everything I want. I love you, and I want you in my life,” he pleaded.

She looked at him. For a moment, she felt pity for him. He looked so tortured. Then she remembered who he was: George! He was merely putting up an act. She rose.

“I think you should go home with your parents,” she said and walked out of the big sitting room.

CHAPTER 29

Boma remained in her room and did not have breakfast with her family that Sunday morning. Her parents were not pleased with her with the sad outcome of the previous day's lunch with the Douglases. Not a word was said to her when George and his parents left but from the looks on her parents' faces, she could tell they were angry with her. When she later went downstairs, she realised she was the only one in the house as her family had gone to church. She did not mind. She had breakfast and went to the bathroom.

Thirty minutes later, she was out of the house. She went to Richard's house. She had refused to talk to Tonye the previous evening when she tried to explain herself. To her, Tonye had betrayed her.

Richard did not expect Boma that morning, so he was taken aback when he saw her at the door. He welcomed her. He was alarmed when she told him what had happened. Then, he became visibly disturbed.

"Boma, I have thought about this thing. I should get a transfer and quietly leave this town to maybe the east or the north. I will quickly settle down and then, you will disappear and come to be with me. We will get married quickly and then, there is nothing anybody can do about it," he said.

She cogitated over it. "I think you watch too many western films. My father would declare me missing if he doesn't know my whereabouts and my photograph will be everywhere. I will be found out in no time," she said.

"Then, let's leave the country," he suggested.

She was not sure about his suggestions. She still thought the easier and more sensible thing to do was to just let everybody know what was going on between them. Her family already knew he existed; they just did not know that he was the one; someone they knew so well.

Richard listened to her. He feared what would happen between him and Patrick if his friend found out that he had gone against him by having a romantic relationship with his sister. He was not prepared for that. He could not just hurt his best friend from boyhood. Sopriye still came to his mind but he shook the thought off.

Just then, the doorbell rang. They were startled. He whispered that she should go to the bedroom and remain there because he was not sure who was there. The bell rang again. Boma understood. She went to the inner room while he went to the door.

At the door, Richard peered through the peephole. His heart began to beat very fast when he saw it was Barbara. What did she want? She was with someone whose face was out of view. He was annoyed. What did she want again? He was not ready for her nonsense.

The bell rang yet again. He snorted and ignored it. He went to his bedroom.

Boma stared wild at him. She gestured her query but he shook his head and sat on the bed beside her. The bell rang one more time.

"It's Barbara. I don't know what she is looking for. I have told her I'm not interested in her but she keeps disturbing my life," he said.

Boma was quiet. She was annoyed that Barbara was still coming to see Richard. Though she did not want to doubt him, she did not understand why she would still be coming to him when he had told her he was not interested. Maybe there was something he was not telling her because she could not imagine herself going to a man's house when he did not want her and had told her not to.

She looked at him and sneered in disgust.

"What is it?" he asked.

She shook her head. It was another battle going on in her head. What if this reputed player was actually playing with her emotions? What if he was just catching his grooves with her? Though she was sure of his position with Barbara as she had heard from her brother, what she did not understand was why Barbara kept coming to see him.

Richard knew she was not happy because it was his ex at the door. "But you know I have nothing with Barbara?"

"I don't know anything," she snapped and got up. "Anyway, I have to be home before my father starts looking for me. He thinks I am still in my room."

"Boma, please," he said. He understood that she was cutting short her visit.

She got up and walked to the living room en route exiting the house. He walked behind her. At the door, he held her hand. She turned to only give him a glance and turned away. "It's okay," she said and wriggled her hand from his hold. She opened the door and left.

Richard was unhappy. He blamed Barbara for Boma's anger. He would have to warn Barbara, and sternly so, never to come to his house. He was over with her and she must accept that. He slumped on his couch with a broken heart. Boma was hurt and that hurt him too. Just then, what she had told him happened the previous day hit him. He jumped up! He was almost tremulous as he thought of the possibility of Boma succumbing to the pressure of her parents to go to George. He was instantly alarmed.

Boma's anger had abated by the time she got home. She had reasoned that she had reacted unfairly to Richard. She would have to see him again later that evening. Just as she got home, she met Tonye standing outside in the vast compound, admiring a beautiful new car. She wondered which visitor was around again.

Tonye saw her and smiled. Boma did not return the smile. She walked towards the house.

"Boma," Tonye called cheerfully. "Come and see your car."

Boma was shocked. Her car? She stopped and turned around. She did a mental check; it was not her birthday. She walked towards the car and her sister with a puzzled grimace. "It's not my birthday, why then did Daddy buy a car for me?" she asked. Just as she said it, she suspected that it was because she had just become a graduate. But her father did not buy a car for any of her elder siblings when they became graduates.

Tonye's smile broadened and she looked genuinely happy. "You are so lucky, Boma, to have a gift like this."

It was a very beautiful car. She could see the exotic interior and she marvelled at its magnificence. "Why did Daddy buy me a car?" The last time she saw her father, he was angry with her and had refused to talk to her.

"It's not Daddy who bought you the car. It is from George," Tonye blurted out excitedly. "Aren't you lucky?"

Boma hissed, suddenly disliking the car. She turned and stormed away towards the house. She was in flight on the staircase when she heard her brother's voice. She turned and saw him smiling at her.

"Congratulations, Boma," Abiye said.

She frowned. "For what?" she demanded, her tone aggressive.

"Your brand new, beautiful car. You have such a car when you've not even worked for a day."

"I don't have any car," she said and ran up the stairs to her room.

Her brother entered her room a few seconds later. He looked puzzled. "Didn't you see that flashy car outside?" he asked. "That is the latest model of Lexus GS350."

She was silent for a moment. Then she nodded. He told her it was from George and his parents.

"Why are they giving me a car? What did I do to deserve it? I don't want anything from them."

Abiye sat beside her and put his arm around her shoulder. "Boma, stop being hard on yourself! This guy and his folks love you and it is obvious. Then, they are friends of Daddy and Mummy. His mother is Mummy's best friend from secondary school," he said.

She looked at him. "Abiye, do you have such a friend who has been your best friend from secondary school?" she asked, a sudden ray of hope beaming in her eyes.

Abiye thought for a moment and nodded. "I have few of them. Richard is one of such friends," he said.

"Good! Now, imagine that Richard whom you say is a best friend from secondary school comes here to say he wants to marry one of your sisters. What will you do? Will you say because he's your friend, you must support him?"

Abiye chewed over it for a moment. He shrugged. "They are not the same scenarios. My friend cannot marry my sister. It is different from my friend's son marrying my daughter. It is sacrilege for my friend to marry my sister," he said.

Her heart fell. "They are the same issues. George is not a good person. He is a thug, a notorious serial skirt-chaser and a shameless heartbreaker," she said.

"I understand and you said so but he is repentant and has shown remorse. You have nothing to lose," Abiye said.

She had thought that her brother was on her side but it seemed the car gift had changed his stance. She was sad.

Just then, Tonye came to the room and told Abiye that he had visitors. He asked who they were.

"Your girlfriend and Barbara," Tonye said.

Abiye was excited. He jumped up to his feet. "Boma, come and see my delectable woman," he said and dashed out.

Tonye stared at Boma. She came to her and sat beside her. Boma got up almost immediately.

"Boma, I am sorry if you are still angry with me. But see, George is for real," she said.

"Then go and marry him," Boma snapped at her and walked out of the room. She went down. She wanted to quickly meet Abiye's girlfriend. The fact that Barbara was there gave her some shivers but she braced herself; after all, she was in her father's house.

Barbara was excited to see Boma. She got up and hugged her. "How are you, Boma? Wow! You look as beautiful as ever," she said.

Boma smiled. Barbara too was as beautiful as ever. Boma admitted that she was a sweet lady and she wondered why such a stupendous beauty could not move on with her life rather than chase after Richard who had lost interest in her.

She greeted her warmly and it was like she had not been angry because of her a while ago.

Boma looked around. There was no other lady in the room. "Where is your girlfriend?" she asked Abiye.

"She is in the restroom," he said, a finger nodding towards the direction of the visitor's toilet. "She will be out soon."

Boma turned to Barbara. Barbara was still smiling at her with sheer admiration in her eyes. "How have you been?" she asked in need of something to say.

Barbara heaved, expelling a hard sigh. "My dear, it has not been easy. I have been battling heartbreak," she answered.

Boma gave her a deliberate concerned look. "What happened?" They sat on a sofa next to each other.

"The guy I fell so helplessly in love with doesn't want me. He is a heartbreaker, who plays with women's emotion, but I am deeply in love with him and cannot afford to lose him. He has been acting very difficult," Barbara said.

Boma shook her head in pity. "Then, why are you hurting yourself? Don't let any man keep you suffering under his spell. You know who he is, so why waste your life with him. You should forget about him and move on," she said.

"I have tried to but I can't. I just love the guy. I don't even mind proposing to marry him if he would not propose to me," Barbara said ridiculously.

Boma suddenly believed that it was not possible because Richard would never accept her. "Barbara, don't keep hurting yourself. You have stupendous values, cherish yourself and leave the guy. Such a guy doesn't deserve you," she said. "Look at you, you are beautiful, you are sophisticated and you are intelligent. Why hold on to a man who does not want to be held at all?"

Just then, the door of the visitor's toilet opened and Abiye's girlfriend emerged. Boma, out of curiosity, turned to see the girl. She was shocked and alarmed. She got up instantly, her jaw dropped.

"Boma!" the lady said, equally shocked. "What are you doing here?"

"This is my father's house," Boma muttered as she stared in disbelief.

CHAPTER 30

Tombra could not believe it that Abiye was Boma's brother. She was not sure what to expect from Boma. She went to her and was relieved when Boma smiled at her and hugged her.

Abiye and Barbara were shocked. "You know each other?" Abiye asked.

"We went to the same school," Tombra said. "Boma was the most beautiful girl in the whole school and I can vouch in the whole continent as well."

Boma was disappointed in her brother's choice. Tombra was not the right girl for any man. She was too loose and wayward; she was a fortune-hunter. Girls who dated men for money were after fortunes.

"It is such a small world," Barbara said. She turned to Boma who had now sat again. "Jessica is my first cousin. She moved to Lagos earlier in the year and she is now working in a bank."

Boma smiled. However, she was thinking if to warn her brother against her or not. She was also reasoning that she might have changed from her bad ways. There was no need making a storm in a teacup.

"Jessica?" she turned to Tombra. "Your name is Jessica?"

Tombra smiled. "Yes, I am also Jessica. I know you know me as Tombra. That is still my name and I answer to it."

Abiye smiled. "If your name is Tombra, I would rather call you that than an English name," he said. They laughed.

Just then, the glass door to the living room slid open and lo and behold, Richard walked in. Boma's heart froze. Why was he here?

Abiye jumped up excitedly. "Richie Boy! You're welcome. Come and meet my sweetheart."

Richard was frozen at the door. He stared in both shock and sheer confusion. What was happening? Barbara was there with Boma and that same girl from Boma's school he had met at the airport. Barbara's eyes glistened with joy as she saw him.

"Hey! Hi!" Tombra greeted excitedly. "I remember you! Good to see you."

Abiye and Barbara were shocked as they exchanged puzzled looks. Boma knew the worst was about to happen and all she could do was to wait for it.

"Do you know him too?" Abiye asked her.

"Of course, I do. He used to come to Port Harcourt. Is he not Boma's boyfriend? I know him," Tombra said.

Abiye was dazed and so was Barbara.

"What? No, it's not possible!" Abiye shouted and stared daggers at his friend.

Richard had only come around because Boma had left his house in anger and he was afraid that she could start considering George. He wanted to find a way to get to her. Now, this was the big disaster! However, he would not deny it now that he had been exposed. "Patrick, take it easy and hear me out," he said.

Barbara was staring at Boma in shock. Boma was embarrassed and could not look at her. She was like a child who had been caught stealing red-handed.

"What do you want me to hear? That you are such a snake and have been going behind my back to have an affair with my sister?" Patrick barked at him.

"I need you to understand. I won't deny it. I was only looking for an opportunity to tell you. I love Boma and what I feel for her is real. I love her with everything that I am worth," Richard said.

Abiye stared at him indignantly. He felt like physically assaulting him. "How dare you? She is my sister for goodness sake and you call yourself my friend," he howled at him.

Tombra was confused. Why was Abiye so angry?

"I am your friend," Richard said.

"No, you are not. You are a snake. I shouldn't have brought you close to my family," Abiye said.

Just then, Tonye walked in. She had heard her brother's angry voice. "What is going on here?" she asked.

"This evil spirit here has been secretly molesting Boma," Abiye wailed.

"What?" Tonye shouted in shock as she turned to Richard in outrage..

"Stop it!" Boma suddenly screamed. "He has not been molesting me and has never. He loves me, yes, and I love him too. What is wrong in that?"

A shock wave went through the room.

"It's true. They are in love," Tombra said.

"You, shut up!" Boma barked at her. That compounded her confusion.

Tonye would not digest it. "You're in love with Richard? Where and when did that start?" she asked.

"Love starts from anywhere," Boma said.

Tonye turned to Richard. "You must be ashamed of yourself. I thought you called Abiye your best friend and you are secretly dating his sister when you know you will always break her heart."

"I will never do that to Boma," Richard said.

Barbara suddenly broke down and began to weep. Tombra was further confused. What's really happening here?

"So that is why you have been avoiding me and rejecting my pleas," Barbara said amidst her tears, pointing an angry finger at Richard.

Richard looked away.

Abiye was staring angrily at him. It was rather inconceivable that his best friend had been having an affair with his sister. It was abominable to him for any boy to have an affair with his friend's sister. Even if that happened, it should not be someone like Richard who was wayward and reckless with girls' emotions. He was very angry.

"What are you still doing here?" Abiye demanded harshly. Richard looked at him apologetically. "Get out of here and I don't ever want to see you in this house or anywhere near my sisters!"

Richard looked at Boma. She walked across the room to him. Abiye grabbed her arm and pulled her back roughly. She struggled.

"Don't hurt her, Patrick," Richard said.

"Get out of here!" Abiye thundered.

Richard did not move. He looked at Boma. "Boma, don't worry, nobody can quench the fire of our love. I will never stop loving you," he said.

"He said you should get out!" Tonye said, her voice raised.

Richard turned to Tonye. "There is nothing wrong in loving Boma," he said.

Abiye was too furious. He rushed towards him and pushed him roughly in his chest, ordering him out. Tonye and Tombra held him back, pleading with him not to fight.

Boma was sad; tears had begun to run down her cheeks. "Richard, please go. I will see you later," she begged.

"Leave him! Let him stay and see just how I will spill his wretched blood. Look at him, he has nothing. Is it not George who just delivered a brand new car to you today? Does this idiot have anything other than that rickety second hand car that has seen better days?" Abiye howled at him in sheer frustration and anger.

Richard sighed. He turned around and walked out. This was the evil day he had always dreaded. He went home, his mind in turmoil.

"Boma, how could you?" Abiye turned his anger to his sister. "I warned you against that silly guy. He is no good and I was trying to protect you. Why did you allow him to deceive you?"

Boma was annoyed now. "He did not deceive me. He is a nice and loving guy and I love him," she said defiantly.

"Boma, you don't know him," Tonye said. "Richard is no good. I cannot advise my worst enemy to have anything to do with him because in the end, he would wreak havoc. Barbara is here. She is his victim. She is still crying over him but he has moved on to you and whoever else."

Barbara rose. She was wiping her tears away now. "Boma, in case you do not know, Richard is the man I was talking about. I still love him and want him back," she said, fresh tears running down her face.

Boma felt guilty that she was responsible for her tears. "I am sorry if he is the one, but you see, Richard and I are in love and I can't help you," she said. She turned to Tombra who was surprised that Richard was the same boyfriend her cousin had just taken her to his place about an hour ago. "Tombra, you see that? Everywhere you go, you take destruction with you. Don't think you will get in here so easily." She stormed out of the room, hurt with tears flying in her eyes. For her, the die was cast.

CHAPTER 31

Boma's parents were brutally stunned, disappointed, and angry when Abiye had reported Boma and Richard to them. Her father shared his son's sentiment that it was utterly wrong for Richard to have any affair with Boma because of his friendship with Abiye.

He immediately summoned Boma and the reproach was heavy and harsh. Her family was completely against her relationship with Richard and her father ordered that whatever she had with Richard must end immediately.

Boma broke down and wept. It incensed her father who was at sea at why she was weeping.

"Stop that nonsense! What are you crying for? With what Richard has done, going behind your brother to commit such a social aberration should tell you that he cannot be trusted," her father said.

"How could Richard do this?" Boma's mother wondered aloud. She shook her head in disappointment.

"The worse problem is that he has a penchant for making girls love him and then, he breaks their hearts," Abiye said, an overdose of spite evident in his voice.

"Boma," her father's voice boomed, "did you hear what I've said? You must end whatever relationship you have with that boy." It was an order he apparently expected obedience without hesitation.

Then Boma shocked every one of them. "I can never stop being with him. He loves me and I love him; that is all that matters," she said. "I would rather leave this house to be with him."

Her parents exchanged stares. Tonye could not believe that Boma could say that to her parents.

"Boma, wake up, Richard does not love you or any girl for that matter. He just plays with women's emotions," her sister said.

"You will not see that boy and you will not leave this house," her mother said. She was very upset with her. "You have George who loves you truly. I mean, see what he just did; he bought you a brand new car."

"I don't want his car. I don't want him. George is the worst man for me. I can never love him," Boma said in frustration amidst her sobs.

Her father was quiet now. He was staring incredulously at her, probably having difficulty to take in what she had said and was saying.

"Richard has brainwashed you. He has nothing to offer you. He will only give you pains, misery, and heartbreak," Abiye said.

"You hate Richard now because he is your friend who is in love with your sister. Yes, he may be a devil, but you must have heard that the devil you know is better than the angel you don't know. You all don't know George. He is a worse devil," Boma said.

"I will hear no more of such nonsense!" her father suddenly bellowed. "I forbid you to see Richard."

Fresh tears cascaded down Boma's face. She was heaving and stifling the urge to break down. She swirled around on her heels and began to charge away. At the door, she stopped and turned around. "Abiye, go and ask Tombra to tell you what she said to me the last time we spoke in Port Harcourt and why she said what she said." She exited the room and ran up the stairs, overwhelmed and now weeping bitterly.

Later that evening, Abiye went with his father to see George's parents who were still in Lagos. It was to thank them for the car gift to Boma.

"I really hope your daughter softens towards my son. He is suffering because of her," Ambassador Douglas said. They were sitting in his private sitting room which was in the pent house.

"Don't worry, she is my child and she has no choice but to do as I tell her," Dr. Horsfall said. Then he told his friend what had happened and how they had discovered the misery boyfriend to be Abiye's close friend, Richard.

"The snake was sneaking behind his friend to Port Harcourt to see my daughter. Abiye here had no idea that he was going to see his sister in Port Harcourt," Boma's father said.

George's father was pleased to see that both Boma's father and her brother were against the relationship between Richard and Boma. He suggested that they must think of how to destroy the relationship irrevocably. It was a surge of exhilaration that welcomed their acceptance of his suggestion.

"We have to shock Boma by making him look horribly unacceptable. What do you think?" George's father suggested.

"Anything that will make my daughter hate him is fine with me. I don't approve of him. Such a character cannot be trusted," Boma's father said.

George's father's eyes moved to Abiye for his position. Abiye nodded in alignment with his father. The former federal minister smiled. “I am a politician to the core. I know just how to fix this up and it will be just fine,” he said.

***

Boma did not come down for supper. She remained locked up in her room. Tonye decided to take her food to her in the room but Boma turned her back, refusing to open the door. Somehow, she was most disappointed in Tonye. She expected that, if everyone was against her, Tonye would attempt in the least to understand her better but, unfortunately, she did not offer her that sisterly support.

Boma remained in the room, nurturing her broken heart and considering her next line of action. She would never stay away from Richard. She would do anything to be with him. She was frustrated that everyone on her family took it as an abomination for her and Richard to be in love simply because he was Abiye’s friend. He was not a relative for goodness sake!

She must have slept off afterwards because the rapid knocking at the door woke her up with a start. She wondered who it was. The knock continued.

“Boma, I am sorry. I think I over-reacted. I need to have a word with you and seek your forgiveness,” her brother’s voice floated in.

She was surprised. Had her brother had a rethink? She had a glimmer of hope. She went to the door and opened it.

Abiye stepped in, looking at her with dark eyes; her own eyes searching his face.

"Why are you doing this to yourself?" he asked, and that instant, she knew he had tricked her.

"What do you want?" she asked.

"You can't keep being hard on yourself simply because the people who love you the most are trying to protect you from unnecessary hurt and future regret," he said.

"Nobody should protect me. I am not a baby. I know what I want?" she said, annoyed that he had come here to say this to her.

He sat on the only chair in the room. "You don't know that guy called Richard. He is not a good person. He is wicked. He is a rogue. Let me tell you something you don't know about him. Back in university, he was moving with some boys who were later arrested for robbery. They indicted him but, somehow, he was able to escape because he had an uncle who was a police officer. Things got missing whenever he was around and people saw him as a thief," Abiye said.

Boma stared at her brother, outraged. "Don't tell lies against a good man. Richard is nice; beautiful in and out," she defended.

Abiye smirked. "No, he is double-faced. He has a criminal record he hides. Is that who you want? A criminal?"

Boma sniggered. "Don't give a dog a bad name to hang it. If he is a criminal, how come he is your friend? Why did you bring him home?"

Abiye was not sure what next to say. He appeared lost for a few moments. "Anyway, I think you should know that Richard is not a good person. He is unfeeling, he is a pretender and he had a dark chequered past."

"I don't care what he has been. All I care about is what I see of him, what I know of him and what I feel about him," she said. "Please, you may take your leave now. I have to go to bed."

Abiye regretted that he had assumed he was smart enough to quickly convince her against Richard and he had not planned well. Now, he had only fooled himself with his shallow allegations and she was not fooled in anyway.

"Just one more thing," he said. "You said something about Tombra this afternoon. What exactly did you mean when you said I should ask her what she said to you the last time you met in PH?"

Boma stared straight at him, her eyes burning with the indignation she felt towards him. "Abiye, go and ask her. She knows George, too, and very well. From that question, you will know a thing or two about George and also about her," she said.

"Talk to me. What did she say? What do you know about her that you think I should know?" he asked. He was bothered about that.

She shook her head. "She is your girlfriend and it is your relationship. It is none of my business," she said.

"But you are my sister and you should tell me things that affect me," he said.

"No," she retorted. "I should mind my business just the same way you should mind your business and tear your eyes away from my affairs."

"Boma, talk to me," he pleaded.

"No!" she hollered impatiently. "Please, excuse me!"

Abiye was angry now. He glowered at her. Then, suddenly, a thought hit him. Boma was possibly trying to ruffle him as a way to get back at him. He snorted and walked out of the room. She slammed the door behind him, a way to send a message to him that she did not expect his return.

Abiye climbed down the stairs leisurely and sauntered into the living room where his father was waiting. The man looked at him with an enquiring expression. Abiye shook his head.

"She did not buy it," he said.

CHAPTER 32

Richard knew he was in big trouble when he arrived at the bank's headquarters and was ushered into the General Managing Director's office. He had been summoned to report there at exactly a quarter to noon. He had never had any business with the General Managing Director and he was unsure as to why the big man whom every member of staff dreaded so much would send for him. Many thoughts ran through his head but he kept hope that all was fine. He got there five minutes earlier, and just as he entered the large office on the top floor of the high rising building and saw the two men with the GMD, he knew there was trouble.

He recognised Ambassador Douglas and of course, he knew Boma's father very well. They sat leisurely opposite the GMD's desk, glasses of champagne sat before them on the expansive, padded desk. The GMD sat staring directly at him as he entered the office. He made to greet the men but Boma's father's eruption botched his attempt.

“This is the filthy imbecile who is molesting my daughter,” Boma’s father yelled angrily at him.

Richard was taken aback because he did not expect such attack from Boma’s father whom he had always seen as a gentleman.

“Are you Richard?” the GMD, a lanky elderly man with a foxy face that revealed intolerance for trivialities asked him in his habitually commanding voice.

“Yes, sir,” Richard answered, slightly bowing.

“Do you know what molesting someone’s daughter can do to you? Do you know what it can do to the image of this establishment since you are a member of staff here?” the GMD asked.

Richard sighed, staring at all the men in the long view that where he stood afforded him. “I have not molested anybody’s daughter, sir,” he answered.

“Will you shut up?” Boma’s father raged. “What did you do to my daughter? I sent her to school to study and you left your job to travel all the way to Port Harcourt to profane her innocent mind to be in love with you. And you were pretending to be a friend of my family.”

“I am sorry if you are angry with me for falling in love with your daughter, sir. I genuinely love her; and she and I have found our chemistry in each other,” Richard said. He had quickly decided to be calm and clear headed because whatever impression he created to the GMD would determine his fate, which for now, was hanging precariously in the balance.

Boma's father stared daggers at him. "You are sorry? Good, I will accept your sorry if you desist from having anything to do with my daughter. If not, I am ready to make your life unbearably miserable," he said.

George's father took a swig from his glass and smiled mischievously, he tilted his head and watched on, gratified.

Richard's eyes moved from the GMD who was watching the spectacle, then to George's father who seemed happy and then back to Boma's father. "I have promised Boma that I will never leave her no matter what. She had anticipated all this would happen, especially after Ambassador Douglas here offered me money to leave her and I told him she was worth more than all the money in the world," he said. He wanted Boma's father to know what had truly happened and how he was not ready to fail Boma.

Boma's father was not interested in what he said. "Are you saying you will not leave my daughter alone? Even when I tell you to do so?" he asked, his eyes burning with what looked like hate.

"I am sorry, sir. I am irredeemably in love with Boma and whatever woe that would befall me because of my decision to be true to her, I will accept it in good fate but I will not turn my back on her," Richard said. He wondered where he had derived all the guts to tell the elderly man that and in front of the GMD whom he knew not what was going on in his head. Whatever trouble, even if it would mean losing his job, he would take it.

George's father shook his head. "Young man, you shouldn't always show your lack of home training. At least, courtesy demands that you should listen to elders. The man says leave his daughter alone, you are insisting you'll not. Do you know you could get into trouble for this bad behaviour? If anything happens to his child, can you stand the trouble? Look elsewhere for another girl where you will be accepted."

Richard deliberately kept mute for a long minute, staring at the men. The GMD sat back on his chair, swivelling from side to side and staring at him. His face was expressionless. Richard was sure that the man would order his relief from the bank.

"With all due respect, sir," Richard finally began, "maybe your reason for offering me five million naira to leave Boma for your son is what is behind your reprimand. I am sorry, sir; it won't work."

George's father was incensed as a sudden fury burnt in his eyes. He flared up. "What insolence! What imprudence! How dare you speak to me like that? Do I look like your mate? Do you know who I am in this country?" he thundered, threateningly.

The GMD rose. "Ambassador, calm down, please," he pleaded.

"No, you need to discipline this recklessly disrespectful urchin. How dare he?" the former ambassador raved on.

The GMD turned to Richard. "You! Go and wait for me in the reception," he barked.

"He should be sacked at once," Boma's father howled.

"Please, calm down, the bank's disciplinary committee will look into his matter and make recommendations," the GMD said.

Richard left the office and went to the reception. His hands were trembling from anger. He understood what the two men were out to do against him. They wanted to throw him out of his job. He shrugged. One thing he knew was that he would never betray Boma by leaving her, regardless of the pressure.

He was at the reception waiting for more than one hour before the GMD finally came out with his visitors. They did not seem to notice him in the reception because he was sitting at the far end of the hall. They walked out of the reception. Apparently, the boss was seeing the men off. Richard waited patiently. He was prepared for the worst.

Shortly, the boss returned and was en route to his office when Richard rose and moved towards him. The GMD saw him and raised a brow. He gestured for him to follow him.

Richard's heart was pounding hard. He would face a tough time with the boss, he was sure of that.

The GMD went straight to his seat and offered Richard a seat where the visitors had vacated. He took it, wondering what the man was up to.

"Ambassador Douglas is a big customer of our bank; he's been for years so you understand the importance of such a man of his status. We hold him in high esteem. Dr. Horsfall holds shares in this bank. I hope you understand the implication of this," the GMD said surprisingly soft spoken.

Richard nodded. "Yes, sir," he said.

"They want to deal with you and they want you sacked from this bank. Whatever they want, we will have to oblige them. They want you to stay away from the girl in question, so you can keep your job," the boss said. He seemed to regret giving such explanation.

Richard shrugged when he noticed the man had paused and was staring at him.

"You know, I like the fact that you know what you want. I love men like you who believe in whom they love and they are ready to die for the person. I had similar experience in my time," the GMD said. He picked his moustache and rolled the thick, rough hair at the edge. "My father in-law, a magistrate, threatened me with prison to leave his daughter whom I love so much but I refused and was ready to face hell and high waters for her. In the end, love triumphed. It will be a very bumpy ride for you but just hold on. You can never go wrong when love is true."

Richard thought he was in a dream. This same GMD who inspired fear in workers was the same man talking to him like a doting father. Tears welled up in his eyes.

"Thank you, sir," he said.

"Don't worry; you won't lose your job. Just remember that I had an experience that was much worse, which time will not permit me to tell you. Think of all imaginable sufferings you can; I suffered it and I came out triumphant," the GMD said.

Days passed. Richard did not see Boma because her father had forbidden her from leaving the house. The man had given stern orders to the security man at the gates not to allow her out of the house. She was grounded. Richard was worried because he did not know what had happened to her. He did not want to be too far from her. He had the telephone number of her house but he was afraid to call for fear of it being answered by his parents or siblings. After more than a week, he decided to go to her house one evening.

He was on his way when his eyes caught something. He saw George's father coming out of his car in front of a fancy restaurant. The man was alone. Richard pulled his car off the road. Perhaps, if he went to talk to the man, he could make him understand why he should forget having Boma for his son. He tinkered with the thought for a while.

He got out of the car and crossed the road to the other side. He was about to enter the restaurant when he suddenly thought, *To what end would talking to the man be?* He sighed. The man was desperate to have Boma for his son and so was his wife and now, even Boma's parents because of old friendship ties. It would do him no good.

He was about to turn away and return to his car when he noticed Barbara's car parked in the premises. Was Barbara in the restaurant? He wanted to flee; in fact, he was actually in flight when a better part of him stopped him. What if George's father had found his way to Barbara and they were there to conspire against him? He decided to go in there.

At the door of the restaurant, he scoured through the expansive hall. At the right end, he saw George's father sitting with his back against him and in front of him was that girl who burst the bubble about him and Boma. Sitting beside George's father was Barbara. She was sitting close and leaning on the big man and he had his arm around her. He was baffled.

That position was too compromising. His suspicion quickly formed. He knew Barbara was into big men, a reason why he had failed to love her and stay with her. Did it mean that George's father was having an affair with her? He wondered.

He sauntered leisurely towards the table they were sitting. They were engrossed in their discussion. Tombra was saying something and Barbara was still nestling in Ambassador Douglas' body. He heard the man chuckle at what Tombra said, which he did not hear.

"Baby, you should understand how lonely it is here, take me to London on my next leave," Barbara said, sitting up and running her fingers on the elderly man's face.

Tombra froze as her eyes caught Richard standing behind the man and her cousin. She was now frantically trying to signal Barbara who was not paying attention to her. Richard deliberately walked past them to the east end of the restaurant. He looked out through the window as if he was expecting somebody.

When he turned around, Barbara had changed seats and was now sitting with Tombra. He did not mind them. He was happy that he had seen them and had discovered that George's father was having an affair with Barbara. He could get dirty with the man if the man was still bent on hunting him down because of Boma.

"Hi Richard," Barbara said uneasily as he walked towards them.

He grimaced and walked past. He went out of the restaurant and crossed the road to where his car was parked. Now, he had something! He smiled to himself.

CHAPTER 33

Richard parked his car a few buildings away from Boma's house and walked to the house. He kept bracing himself up to go into the house. At the gate, the security man who knew him very well as a friend of the house and did not know what had happened except that Boma's father had instructed him not to allow Boma out of the house, opened the gates and let him in.

Abiye was outside in the compound with an auto mechanic who had been called to check a family's car. He was shocked when he saw Richard entering the gate. He frowned. Instantly, anger surged up in him.

"What do you want here?" Abiye barked, charging towards the gates. "Get out of here. You are not welcomed here."

"Patrick, you can at least hear me out," Richard said.

"I don't want to hear you," Abiye yelled. "Just get out of here!"

Richard looked around in the hope of seeing Boma come out. "Patrick, assuming I am wrong, can I apologise to you being my friend from way back?" he asked.

Abiye pushed him roughly, obviously spoiling for a fight. Richard was calm. He looked around again, stepping backwards. Then, he saw Boma's father emerge from the house.

"Abiye, don't touch him," the man said to his son. He walked towards them; his bloodshot eyes told Richard that what was to come from him would be harsher than his son.

"What do you want here, young man?" he asked.

"I am sorry, sir. I came to see Boma," he confessed.

The man's anger in his eyes clearly rose but he contained himself. "I told you to leave my daughter alone," he said.

"I am sorry, sir; the love I have for Boma is beyond my control. I am helpless, sir," Richard said.

"Shut your stinking mouth!" Abiye howled at him.

His father raised a hand to stop him. He stared intently at Richard for what looked like eternity and Richard endured it. There was intimidation in the look and it looked like the man would pounce on Richard any moment and rip out his throat.

Pointing at the gates, Boma's father calmly but with apparently weighty command, ordered Richard out. Richard winced for a moment.

"Please, sir, I need to see Boma," Richard pleaded.

Boma's father was shocked by the effrontery. "How dare you?" he asked gently as if he was peeling off from his bewilderment, then all of a sudden, his voice shot up. He bellowed. "Get out of here!"

Richard sighed and allowed his eyes to roam around the compound for a while. Then he walked out. As soon as he got out of the compound, he could hear Boma's father giving strict warning to the gateman not to allow him into the compound again.

Boma could not sleep that night. She was sad that she had been grounded and could not leave the house. It was frustrating because she was not a child. How could her father conceive such obnoxious idea to keep her in the house? It was more or less house arrest and her right to movement was hindered. It was more painful because she could not see Richard. She missed him so much and wondered how he was faring. She knew he would be in a gloomy world, brooding over her.

Her mother had talked with her and she had loosened up and had been having meals but she always returned to her room. Once, she had attempted to sneak out of the house but her elder sister, Tonye, had foiled that attempt. Had she succeeded, she would not have returned home.

Abiye came to talk to her every now and then, he wanted to know more about Tombra and she maintained that his affairs were none of her business and urged him to make hers as none of his business. She knew Tombra had been coming to the house. She had heard her voice once or twice but she never went downstairs to meet her.

Tonye and her father kept away from her. It was good because she was too disappointed in them. That her father would see nothing wrong in her settling for a thug and a serial heartbreaker simply because of some silly friendship broke her heart. She knew ordinarily, her father would have nothing against Richard. George was the reason her father's feelings were tilted against Richard.

"If you call George a thug and a serial heartbreaker, why are you crying over Richard? It looks like hypocrisy to me because Richard is many times over worse. At least, George is repentant; Richard is never remorseful when he wreaks havoc. He's never repentant," Abiye had told her two days ago when he came to talk to her. He was always selling George to her and urging her to forget about Richard.

Boma had suddenly woken up to relieve herself. It was still dark and from the table clock beside her bed, it showed that the time was a few minutes after two am. She had just returned to bed when she heard a voice screaming orders outside her door. The voice was unfamiliar.

She heard a sound of slap and her brother's voice came in a shrill cry. She panicked. What was going on? Then, a hard pounding at her door came.

"Open this door now or I break it down and you're dead," a rough, masculine voice shouted and banged the door again.

That instant, she realised it was a robbery. The robber or robbers were already inside the house. They would break into her room if she did not open the door and they may kill her. Out of sheer fear, she ran to the door and opened it. She saw her brother and father lying on the floor, their heads facing down. There were three armed masked men.

"Step out," the huge man who had banged her down ordered. She was shaking. She obeyed and he asked her who else was in the room.

In a tremulous voice that shook with her entire body, she answered. "Nobody, sir," she said.

The man entered the room for a few seconds and when he returned, he ordered the other men to take them downstairs. Her father and her brother were marched downstairs with her. In the sitting room, her mother and sister were on the floor facing down, with two armed men watching them. They wore masks as well.

"Only three people," one of the men who had brought Boma down reported.

Boma was afraid that the robbers would hurt her family.

They ordered her father and brother to stand. The man who seemed like their leader rose and put his hand around his mouth. "You, Patrick, how would you feel if I shot you and your useless father dead?"

"Please, don't," Abiye begged.

"Give me a reason why I should not," the robber said. He was obviously making noticeable effort to distort his voice. Despite herself, Boma realised that and she thought it must be someone who knew her family and whom her family knew.

"You are pompous because you have beautiful sisters. You think I care about your sisters? I don't!" the robber said and pointed the gun at Boma's father's head.

"Please, don't kill me; I will give you whatever you want?" Boma's father begged.

"Shut up!" the robber said.

"Richie, let's hear him out. He's making an offer. If he gives us good money, we could spare his life," another of the robbers said.

The leader was quiet for a long moment, obviously chewing over it. "How much do you have in this house right now?" he asked.

"I have about one point five million naira," he said.

The leader turned to one of his men. "Go and get the money," he said. The man led the elderly man out of the living room.

"You may all relax. We want money and since your father is giving us money, you will all be spared," a third man said. By now, the leader was sitting on a couch, staring angrily at Abiye.

There was terrible tension in the house. Nobody moved despite the assurance. Minutes later, Boma's father returned with the robber who was carrying a suitcase. He ordered Boma's father to lie down. Only Abiye remained standing.

"Richie, we've got the money. Let's go," the one with the case said.

"I have an axe to grind with this boy but let's leave it for another day," the leader said. They left. Boma could hear their footsteps as they ran out in the dark. It was like a dream. The moment they left, Abiye ran to lock the door.

The family got up. They were all shaking and visibly frightened.

"Let's call the police," Abiye said.

"Calm down. We need to calm down," his father said.

Boma looked at her father. He looked so old and frail; and tortured. Her sister and mother too were frightened. This was the first time they were ever having a robbery experience.

“It seems like the man talking is someone we know,” Tonye said in spite of herself.

“I think so too,” her father said. “But I cannot place the voice. He was making effort to alter the voice.”

“They called him Richie,” Boma’s mother said.

Boma’s father was quiet for a long moment. “Who’s Richie? We don’t know anybody called Richie,” he said with a sigh. His wife and daughter were still frightened to death.

“Richie is short for Richard,” Tonye said.

“Who’s Richard again?” Boma’s father asked. He walked to the window and peered into the darkness toward the gates. The light in the compound had been turned off.

“Richard is Abiye’s friend,” Tonye said.

Boma’s father paused and looked at them in disbelief. Boma was thinking of what her brother had said about Richard being a criminal.

"No, it can't be Richard. Richard, we must give it to him, is a gentleman incapable of such lowlife atrocities as robbery," her father said.

Tonye took a deep breath and exhaled noisily.

"Abiye, come with me. Let's go to the gates. Isn't the gateman there? How did the robbers get into the house?" his father said.

The men went out. Many riotous thoughts were running in Boma's head. Could it be Richard who had come to rob them? He called her brother Patrick which was what he usually called him. He accused Abiye of being pompous because he had beautiful sisters and he said he did not care about his sisters. Obviously, he had an axe to grind with Abiye. Her ears were hot and she felt her head would explode.

Tonye was now pacing about. Clearly, she was trying to solve the puzzle. Her mother was asking them if they were okay. Boma was hoping fervently that it was not her own Richie! But every thought that came to her head led to him.

Her father and Abiye returned.

"The robbers tied the gateman up and a robber was there with him while we were being robbed," her father said.

"The robbers hid their faces because they are people we know and from the way the leader talked, it is clear that he knows me. He called my name. I think they were here to inflict disaster had Daddy not offered them money," he said.

"Richard is the person behind it all. He wanted to deal with us for stopping him from being with Boma. He hasn't broken her heart yet," Tonye said.

"I said it can't be Richard," her father dismissed it.

"Richard calls Abiye by his English name," Tonye said. "And he said Abiye is being pompous because he has beautiful sisters; except Abiye knows another Richie who calls him Patrick."

She had just re-echoed Boma's thoughts and that made Boma more scared.

"I don't know any other Richard," Abiye said.

His father still looked doubtful. Tonye seemed sure. "Remember he was here yesterday evening and you and Daddy sent him away," she said.

Boma was astonished to hear that. She looked up at the men. Even at that, she remained mute, the riot in her head not abating or easing her confusion.

"Let's go back to sleep. In the morning, Abiye and I will go to the police station," her father said.

Boma was distraught now. How could it be Richard? Her brother had alluded that he was a criminal who had been indicted for robbery when they were in school. She rose and walked to where the robber had sat. She wanted to smell the chair if it had the faintest of his fragrance. She knew how he smelt.

Abiye was watching her as she went to the chair. His mother's eyes too caught Boma's movement. Just as Boma got there, she tried to smell around. She needed to convince herself that it was truly Richard who was there. She saw an ID card on the floor beside the chair. She picked it up and looked at it. She froze. All her fears were confirmed. Her heart shattered instantly as she stared wild at the identity card in disbelief.

Abiye went to her and took the ID card from her. He looked at it and screamed. "He's the one! His ID card dropped."

"Who?" his father asked.

Abiye gave his father the ID card. "Richard of course," he said.

The elderly man looked at the photograph and he appeared stunned. "What? It's true?" he uttered in absolute disappointment. "Abiye! Is this the kind of friends you keep?"

Boma's mother was confounded that Richard was the culprit. She was also angry that he had done what he did to them. "Call the police at once!"

CHAPTER 34

Richard was in tears as he was accused of robbery and arrested. He pleaded his innocence but all fell on deaf ears. Nobody believed him. All the bits of evidence were put together to nail him. When he was asked to produce his ID card, he began a futile search as he could not find it. He was confused when the police detective investigating the case showed him the ID card and told him it dropped from one of the robbers who was referred to as Richie.

“It’s not me!” he cried, but it was to the winds because nobody believed him. He was thrown into a cell.

Boma was shattered. Her brother made matters worse by reminding her that he had warned her that Richard was no good.

“Now you see that even George is far better. George changed. He became a better person as he matured but you refused to stop seeing him as the boy that he was. Richard is calculative; he is a genius in evil deeds; and see what he has done. He is a criminal. I am not disappointed on one hand because he has always been this way and I am disappointed on the other hand because I thought with his new job, he would have changed," he said.

Boma just wept with a heavy heart. She wished she had listened to all the blaring sirens around her, warning her against Richard. She had only allowed her feelings to take over and now, she was in regrets. She would have to break up with Richard and remove him from her heart and mind. However, George would never be an option to her. His car gift had remained outside and she had not gone near it.

"Can you take me to the police station? I need to give Richard a piece of my mind and break up with him," she said amidst tears.

"You don't need a ceremony to break up with him. You are done with him," Abiye said.

"I still want to face him and warn him to stay away from me," she said.

Abiye heaved a sigh. He accepted and they both went out. He took his car.

At the station, Richard was so downcast and emotionally miserable. He looked at Boma as tears trickled down her face. "You know I cannot do such. I have no bone for such. I can't even conceive such," he said.

The moment Boma set eyes on him, her anger dissipated and somewhere deep in her, she suspected he was innocent. Then what happened? The facts that nailed him were incontrovertible.

“How come one of the robbers called your name? You are the only Richard who calls my brother Patrick and your ID card fell from his pocket,” she said, more tears running down her cheeks.

Richard was knocked for six. It was the first time he was hearing the details. He looked at Abiye who was staring hostilely at him. “Patrick, you have known me the longest time and we have been friends from secondary school, you know me very well. Have you ever seen me as a thief? As someone who would take what isn’t mine much more going to rob?”

Abiye looked away. Boma turned to her brother because she expected a quick answer. She waited but Patrick did not respond.

“Patrick, say something, you know me the most,” Richard pleaded.

“I don’t know you. Don’t ask me stupid questions. All evidence implicates you,” Abiye retorted.

Richard sighed. “But you can vouch for my good character, can’t you?” he asked, heavy-heartedly.

Just then, the DPO walked in. He frowned when he saw Richard behind the counter. Then, he glowered at the policemen at the counter. "Who asked you to bring this dangerous criminal out here? Has he mentioned the names of his gang members and where the guns are and where they got them?"

"No, sir," a constable answered, throwing a salute at the superior officer. "I am sorry, sir."

"Take him back to the cell," the DPO ordered. The constable obeyed him. The DPO turned to Abiye and his sister. "Yes? Who are you?"

"It was our home he and his gang robbed," Abiye said.

The officer relented. "You are Dr. Horsfall's children. Please, we don't allow high profile offenders to receive casual visitors," he said.

Back in the car, Boma was sad. She sat quietly. Richard had been tortured and called a criminal. He did not look like a criminal and the leader of the robber's voice even though he tried to distort it did not sound like Richard. Hearing him now made her sure of that.

"Why didn't you break up with him?" Abiye asked. "You should have told him. That was why we came here in the first place."

"You told me he was a criminal in school and he had friends who had been involved in robberies and he had been implicated before. Why didn't you answer his question when he asked you if you have ever known him to be a thief?" she asked.

Abiye turned away. She noticed his unease, the same he had felt when Richard had asked him the question.

"I didn't answer because I felt pity by his sight but that doesn't take away from what he is. He is no good," he said.

"There is something not right here," she said.

He turned swiftly to look at her. "Something not right like what?" he asked.

"Let's go home," she said.

Meanwhile, shortly after Abiye and Boma left the house, George arrived. Tonye was alone in the sitting room, seeing a movie. She welcomed him pleasantly.

"Where's everybody?"

"Boma and Abiye went out. They didn't tell me where they were off to. Daddy is at work and Mummy went to keep an appointment. So, I'm home alone," she said.

This was the first time George was coming to the house since the car was delivered. He had not seen Boma that day, and today, he came to try to win her now that Richard had been indicted in a robbery case and he was sure Boma would be heartbroken and regret being in love with Richard.

"Learnt your house was robbed in the wee hours of today," he said.

"It is that boy called Richard. It is a shock. He is so handsome and cool that I find it hard to believe he is capable of such atrocities," she said.

"Faces only hide intentions and characters. A man who can do what he did to your brother by going behind him to love his sister is capable of anything. Such a character is worse than a snake," George said. He was staring at her, grinning.

"It is so disappointing," she said.

"Well, I hope Boma realises that she had been deceived by a criminal all along," he said.

"I hope so," she replied. She rose. "What do I offer you?"

"No, don't worry. Merely talking with you, a beautiful gem, is enough for me." He beamed a bewitching smile.

She grinned, flattered. "You are funny," she remarked.

"I am sure Boma did not appreciate the brand new car I bought for her. That car cost me a fortune," he said. "I take care of the girl I love and I have tried my best for your sister but she does not seem ready for me," he said, staring directly into her eyes.

For lack of what better to say, Tonye asked why he said that. "It's just that I wish it was you I gave the car. You are more accommodating and friendlier and you are very beautiful too."

She grimaced. "Oh! Thank you," she said rather caustic. "You have Boma to concentrate on."

He smiled even broader and she could swear she saw a lecherous look in his eyes. "Let's forget about Boma and talk about us. I will rather buy you cars and take you places. I see your eyes and I see how lovely you are," he said.

She got up again. "Erm… George, I don't know how long Boma will be out, so I suggest you come back another time when she is around," she said, disappointed. How could he try to hit on her?

He rose too and closed the gap between them. Tonye stared at him, ill at ease. He placed a hand on her shoulder. "Don't be too shocked, Tonye. You are a beautiful woman and I see deeper beauty in your eyes reflecting your inside. You like me, don't you? You should, because I do more than just like you," he said and a mischievous smile coiled the edges of his mouth. "I love you, Tonye."

She smelt hemp on his breath. She was taken aback. She had no idea that George smoked cigarette much more marijuana. She was alarmed!

“Nonsense!” she said, trying to brace up. She gently slapped his hand off her shoulder and she walked towards the door, a subtle attempt at escaping from that confinement. He moved fast and grabbed her arm. He pulled her towards him. She was horrified. “What do you think you are doing? Get your hands off me!” she shouted at him.

“I want you to love me like I love you,” he said, now holding her upper arms with both hands, making her face him. She was not as big as Boma. She was slimmer and looked feeble in some ways.

“You are hurting me,” she protested.

He kissed her on her mouth and she spat in his face. She began to struggle. He threw her down on the couch. She stared at him, terrified. What was wrong with him? “George! Stop it at once! I am not your mate!”

“Love knows no age,” he said. He seemed to be enjoying what he was doing. “Why are the girls in your family so difficult? Girls struggle to get my attention, they beg me to have an affair with them, but you girls are too stubborn. Why do you resist me? I am the most irresistibly handsome dude around.”

Tonye quickly got on her feet and moved to the edge of the couch. “You have done enough. Now, leave or you will get yourself in deep trouble,” she said.

He lunged at her and she ran around the sofa. He looked desperate like a wild animal in heat. It was that moment she regretted that she had not stood with Boma against him. He came after her and she ran around. When she had the opportunity, she ran towards the door. She had reached the slide door when he caught up with her. He grabbed her dress from the back and pulled her roughly. The dress ripped.

"Stop it!" she screamed trying to slide open the door. She expected the gateman to hear her screaming. George grabbed her around her waist and pulled her back in. She was screaming and calling for help. He tried to gag her mouth with his hand. She sank her teeth into his hand and that spilled bile in him.

"You bit me!" he yelled. He hit her across her face. She was dazed. She staggered towards the dining table. She picked up a bottle of whisky which her father had drunk from that morning before leaving. She held the bottle and faced him, one hand holding her torn dress. In her terror, she looked mean and desperate to salvage herself.

"I will kill you! Come a step closer, and I will kill you!" she screamed desperately.

Just then, the door slid open and her father and the gateman entered. They had heard her screaming. Her father who had just returned from his office was alarmed. "What is going on here?" he demanded, horrified by the sight.

CHAPTER 35

Abiye and Boma were stunned when they met a house filled with their parents, Tonye in torn clothes sobbing and being comforted by her mother, and George and his parents. George was kneeling before their father. George's father was appealing to their father while his mother was weeping bitterly with her head in her hands. The first feel of the atmosphere was that something terrible was amiss.

"What is going on here?" Abiye demanded, walking up to Tonye. "What happened?"

His mother looked up at him, and a tear fell from her eye. She pointed at George who was now staring wild and in fear at Abiye. "It's this monster called George," she started but refrained. She recoiled and looked away as if she could not talk again.

Boma lean on the wall by the door. She had already figured the possible situation from the scene. George kneeling, his father talking to her father in an appealing manner and his mother crying; then her sister sad in torn dress sufficed to her what could have happened. Her sad mother and angry father only buttressed her suspicion.

"What happened?" Abiye asked again.

"George tried to have his way with Tonye obviously," Boma said.

Everyone was surprised and turned to her. She smirked at them and shrugged. "Isn't it true?"

"It's true; but how did you know? You were not here," her father said. He looked confused amidst his anger and bewilderment.

"I know George very well. He is a very terrible character. That I rejected him despite all his pleas for more than three years should tell how much and how well I know him. He is a colourless thug, a gutter being without scruples. No matter the gold you wear on a pig, it will always be a pig and return to mud," she said, sounding triumphant.

Abiye was furious. He turned to George. "How dare you come to my house to rape my sister," he screamed and began to charge towards him.

His father stepped forward and stood in his way. "Stop it, Abiye! I will handle this," he said.

"But this is absolute nonsense!" Abiye raved. "He and his parents are begging to have Boma yet he has the temerity to assault my sister!"

"Calm down!" his father pleaded.

Abiye was shaking furiously. That moment, he hated George. "No wonder Boma rejected him. Despite all we were doing for him, he could not use his sense to be good."

"Abiye, please, calm down! Listen to your father," George's father said.

Abiye stared at the man in frustration. Why did he have to make a whimper to him? "I should be calm because he's your son who has assaulted my sister, right?"

"He did not assault her, he only tore her dress," George's father said.

"Excuse me!" Abiye's father said, annoyed. "What do you mean he did not assault her? Tearing her dress is not assault? What was the intention? Was it not to rape her?"

"I am sorry, sir. I don't know what got over me, sir," George pleaded.

"Tonye is even not your mate. You have no respect for anybody, obviously," Abiye said. He charged out of the room.

"I think we should call the police," Boma said.

George and his parents looked at her. She seemed quite relieved that this had happened.

"We can settle it here as family friends," George's mother said.

"Family friends who do not respect the others? What your son has done is a violation of our home, a desecration of the sanctity in our home," she said.

Just then, Barbara and Tombra entered the house. They had heard about the robbery. The moment they entered and saw the scene, they made to leave but it was George's mother who stopped them. "Hey! Come back here. Why are you rushing out?"

They stopped and were confused. George's mother had quickly replaced her tears with anger. "You again?" the woman asked Tombra, pointing at her. "What are you doing here? You followed us from Port Harcourt to Abuja and now to Lagos?"

Frightened, Tombra shook her head. "No, ma," she said in a shaky voice.

George was surprised to see Tombra there. Despite himself, he wondered who the beautiful lady with her was. He was surprised that his mother knew her and wondered what had happened between them.

George's father drooped, exhausted. This was surely a very bad day! He sank into a sofa.

“Why are you harassing her?” Boma’s mother queried George’s mother.

“Ibinabo, this is the girl who has been threatening my marriage for years. She was having an affair with my husband in Port Harcourt and when he went to Abuja, she was organising girls for him there. I have fought with her severally,” George’s mother said.

Everyone was shocked except Boma who had burst into laughter. Tombra was embarrassed. She looked away. Barbara too was uneasy.

“What is funny? Why are you laughing?” her father asked, irritated by her behaviour.

Boma did not stop laughing. “Fine Boy George alias FBG here knows why I am laughing,” she said, casually throwing her hand at George who was now standing with his head bowed.

“Are you not the same girl Abiye brought home as his girlfriend?” Boma’s mother asked in astonishment.

“You better not let your son go anywhere near her,” George’s mother said.

Boma’s mother drew her mouth down in disgust as she looked from Tombra to George’s father, who was sitting slumped and seemingly disconnected from what was happening around him. She hissed and charged towards the door. The ladies moved away to make way for her.

Boma's mother did not go beyond the door. She pushed her head out and called her son's name repeatedly. Abiye came down and into the parlour. He was surprised to see Tombra and Barbara there. He was still upset by what George had done.

"Hi," he said to Tombra, reaching for her arm but his mother slapped off his hand.

"Don't touch her," the woman ordered.

Abiye was confused. "What is happening here again?"

"What is happening here again is that your girlfriend is not a decent girl. She was having an affair with Chief Douglas and his wife here has been having fights with her," his mother said.

Abiye was shocked. He gawked at Tombra in disbelief and he was speechless. Tombra curtsied slightly, a gesture of plea. She was so ashamed. Boma was still laughing.

"She is a wayward girl, very loose and not different from a prostitute," George's mother said.

"Boma, will you stop laughing?" her father retorted. "It is not funny!"

Boma stopped laughing but the grin remained. "It is funny, Daddy. A father and his son have eaten from the same bowl," she said.

There was silence all around. George's mother was the worst hit. She got the message and turned to George.

"You slept with her too?" she asked, outrageous.

Abiye was too weak, embarrassed and ashamed that he had brought home a girl whose dirty linen was being washed before his family. He was also angry that Tombra was that kind of a person. This was what Boma knew about Tombra that she did not want to say. He had asked Tombra about it but she had denied remembering the last time she met Boma in Port Harcourt. He looked at George and his father. He was irritated.

Then, he turned to his father. "We should go and release Richard because he is innocent," he blurted out.

His father shook his head vigorously. "No, no! Don't go there!" he warned.

"Richard did not do anything wrong to be locked up. We know it. We should have him released," he said.

Boma was staring at her brother and wondering what he was saying. George's father got up and told his wife that they must return home.

"You cannot go anywhere," Abiye said angrily. "It was your idea to have Richard behind bars. He is innocent. You must get him out!"

His bemused mother asked what he was talking about. His father told her to ignore him. Tombra and Barbara had taken that opportunity to slip away from the house. Tonye saw them but she ignored. She was still traumatized by what George had tried to do to her.

"Daddy, George cannot come near this family again, never! So he should know that he cannot have Boma again. Richard is locked up because of him," he said. He turned to his mother. "Richard is not a criminal. The robbery was a setup. Daddy and I were involved. It was Chief Douglas' idea. He got the boys to pretend to rob us and pretend one of them was Richard. I have a key to Richard's apartment because I used it sometimes when I have a friend I do not want to bring home. I sneaked into his house and stole his ID card, which we used to nail him," Abiye confessed.

Boma, her sister, and the two women were shocked. Boma's father sighed.

"We did it for this silly monster and look at the mess he and his father have made," Abiye said.

Tears were running down Boma's face. Her poor Richard was just a victim of her own father and brother in connivance with George's father. "Daddy, how could you?"

"I guess I have to say I am sorry. Maybe I was misled," her father said. He too now looked exhausted and worn out as he sank into the sofa that he usually sat on.

“I will go to the police station and make a report that Richard was set up and I will also report that my sister was assaulted by Ambassador Douglas’ son. Afterwards, I will go to the newspapers and tell them this sad story,” Boma said.

“Stop that nonsense! You want to disgrace your father? I said I was misled,” her father hollered.

“You should be ashamed of this,” his wife said angrily. “Do you know the psychological torture I went through because of that robbery incident?” She held Boma’s hand and pulled Tonye. She led them out of the room to her room upstairs.

George’s mother was sad and ashamed. She looked at George with angry eyes. It was obvious that he had blown his chances to ever be accepted by Boma and her family.

“I guess this has ended this way because of your stupid son,” Boma’s father said, his teeth clenched indignantly. “Go and release that boy and take your son away. I don’t ever want to set eyes on him. And take that car out of my compound!”

CHAPTER 36

Richard wiped the tears from his eyes as he looked at Boma, her father, and her brother. It was hard to suck it in that he had been arrested and humiliated because Patrick and his father were against him having anything to do with Boma. A policeman had brought him to their house after getting directives from George's father.

"Richard, we are sorry this happened, I hope you can forgive us," Boma's father said. He heaved a hard sigh. "I allowed my sense of friendship with George's parents to get the better of me. I have nothing against you except that you were going to obstruct our plan to reconcile George and Boma."

Abiye too exhaled noisily. "I have something against you and you know it. Friends don't date their friends' sisters. I don't know why it is like that but it is not a comfortable feeling. Then, I know you too well, you don't keep a girl for long," he said.

Richard just stared at them, heaving. It was obvious that he was not happy.

"Richard, please forgive them for my sake and the love you have for me," Boma pleaded. She walked up to him and wrapped her hands around his body and rested her head on his heaving chest. Richard's eyes could not tear away from Abiye and his father.

"The truth is that I have always liked you. I see you as an upward mobile young man. I feel so ashamed that I allowed myself to condescend to such abysmal level. I am very sorry Richard, my boy," her father said.

Richard drooped. His eyes finally drew away from them and fell on Boma. Again, he wiped the tears that threatened to fall from his eyes. His GMD's voice echoed in his head, *It will be a very bumpy ride for you but just hold on. You can never go wrong when love is true.*

He pulled away from Boma and walked up to Abiye. He stared him straight in the eyes. "Patrick, I have known you almost all my life, from when I was in my first year in secondary school. We were best friends. At university too, we were best friends. You are against me dating your sister because we are friends but you have forgotten something, you dated Sopriye, my cousin who grew up with my family and who is no less a sister to me when we were at university. You went behind me. I knew of it, I never said anything. For you it was a fling, but for her, she fell in love and you broke her heart. I did not even quarrel with you about it. That is because you were my friend; but in your case, I became an enemy for falling in love with your sister, even with genuine intentions," he said.

Abiye drooped. He remembered Sopriye. She was somewhere in the UK studying now. He had met her upon one visit to Richard's family house in Abonnema where he and his friend had gone to spend the holiday. Sopriye was very beautiful and nubile; he learnt that she had an Igbo mother who had deserted her to return to her hometown because of family issues. Her father could not raise her and Richard's father who was her father's brother in-law took her in and raised her like his daughter. She blossomed during maturation and at that time when Abiye met her, she was barely twenty years old. He liked her and was sneaking to talk to her. She fell for him and they had a steaming affair. She was in love and deeply so, but Abiye was only having a good time and it all ended when the holiday ended. She had been hurt and when she learnt that he was seeing another girl in school, she was devastated.

They never met again. Abiye was surprised that Richard knew of this and had never mentioned it to him. The only thing he ever said about Sopriye when he relocated to Lagos was that she was in the UK studying and that she had reunited with her mother. He drooped, ashamed of himself. Richard was a truer friend, he admitted.

"I am sorry," Abiye muttered. "But you and I know you are a heartbreaker; you break hearts of girls who fall in love with you."

"Like you didn't break Sopriye's heart, right?" he asked.

Boma's heart suddenly began to pound rapidly. Was Richard dating her because he wanted to take his pound of flesh from her brother? She was scared but waited. Her father was just listening quietly, his head bowed pensively.

"That was a long time ago and I didn't know you knew of this," Abiye said.

"Patrick, I knew of it. The moment you began to talk to her, I knew. She told me that you were asking her out and I told her you were a nice person and if she liked you, she could accept. I didn't have to tell you all that. My assumptions were that you would respect our friendship and not hurt her. You did hurt her in the end. I did not get mad at you because I did not want to hurt our friendship," Richard said.

He turned to look at Boma, then to her father who was not looking at him, and he returned to Abiye. "Our friendship is nothing now. It is broken and finished. You have rejected me because I fell in love with your sister. Yes, I have broken hearts but why couldn't you give me a chance like I did for you with my cousin?"

"Richard, I have made my mistakes and I have apologised for them," Abiye said.

"I don't accept such apologies. If George did not do what he did, you would not be sorry and I would have been languishing for what I know nothing about. My lawyers will get back to you and your father and all those who were involved. Now, I am ready to fight dirty," Richard said.

Boma's father raised his head swiftly. Richard swirled on his heels and stormed out, Boma running after him and calling his name but he did not answer her. He left in anger.

Boma broke down and wept bitterly. This was the end of their love! She feared and she felt the excruciating pains of heartbreak and the choking feeling of it that came upon her and almost stole her breath. She was distraught.

Tonye who was taking a nap, came out when she heard Boma's voice. She asked what was going on but Boma would not speak. She wept on. Her father rose and left the living room to his room. He looked too exhausted. He must have some regrets now.

Abiye crouched in front of Boma. He was sad and evidently sorry. He took her hands in both hands and squeezed them gently. "Don't cry, Boma, I promise you, I will right all the wrongs, please, trust me," he said.

Boma was helpless, she just wept on.

"I see that Richard loves you for real and I know he will come back for you but before then, I will save two things, my friendship with him and his love for you," he said.

She just looked at him amidst her tears. She did not know how he would do that. He had hurt Richard badly.

***

Boma arrived at Richard's house that afternoon, trepidation all around her. She had been restless all through the previous night. She decided to go to him and beg him. She loved him and had not doubted his innocence. She just could not place the missing link.

Boma was surprised to meet Abiye at Richard's house. They were chatting and having drinks. She rubbed her eyes and her brother smiled at her.

"Abiye! What is happening here?" she asked.

"I am *chilling* with my friend," he answered.

Richard grinned at her. "It is over, Boma," he said. The smile faded off his face and his eyes stared directly into her eyes.

She became nervous. "What is over?"

He smiled again. "The fights, the pains, and all the unnecessary encumbrances," he said.

She almost choked with the instant surge of exhilaration that diffused through her being. She laughed and ran into his arm. He hugged her tight, she held tighter.

"Your brother and I have talked. We have buried the hatchet and everything is now by-gone. I forgive everything that has happened," he said as he pecked the back of her ear. "I always knew that true love will always prevail."

"I love you Richard. You are a beautiful being," she said.

Abiye smiled at them. He rose and came to his sister, his glass of wine in his hand. "Boma, I owe you an apology. I am sorry about the lies I said to discredit my friend. He was not what I said about him. He is not a criminal. You were right when you insisted that something was not right when we left the police station. Actually, everything was not right. He was innocent and knew nothing about what he was accused of."

Boma looked at him. "What about that he is a heartbreaker?" she asked.

He smiled mischievously. "He *was* a heartbreaker," he said.

They laughed. "I am glad all is now over," Richard said. "Let's not talk about the past. We have a future to look forward to."

Boma smiled and hugged him tighter. She just loved him and so much!

Boma's father was glad that Richard had decided to sweep everything under the carpet. He sent for him and apologised again. He promised to always support them. Boma's mother and Tonye too accepted him.

A few weeks later, Abiye returned home to announce that he just learnt that Barbara got married to a politician in Abuja. Boma was very happy for her and indeed for herself and Richard. The storm was finally over for them. The future held sunlight for her and Richard. She smiled brightly as she envisioned the great beautiful future that awaited her and her beau. "*Like a rhyme with no reason, in an unfinished song. There was no harmony, life meant nothing to me, until you came along. And you brought out the colours. What a gentle surprise. Now, I'm able to see all the things life can be, shining soft in your eyes...*" The song played in her head. She had heard the song over and over again; even at home when her father played country songs in the morning. She crooned the lyrics now with a massively joyful heart. Indeed, Richard had decorated her life!

The End

Printed in the USA
CPSIA information can be obtained
at www.ICGtesting.com
LVHW041258151023
761121LV00001BB/182